# ON THE
# RUN

Other Books by Jack Weyland

*Novels*

Charly
Sam
The Reunion
PepperTide
A New Dawn
The Understudy
Last of the Big-time Spenders
Sara, Whenever I Hear Your Name
Brenda at the Prom
Stephanie
Michelle and Debra
Kimberly
Nicole

*Short Stories*

A Small Light in the Darkness
Punch and Cookies Forever
First Day of Forever

*Nonfiction*

If Talent Were Pizza, You'd be a Supreme

JACK WEYLAND

# ON THE RUN

DESERET BOOK COMPANY
SALT LAKE CITY, UTAH

**Library of Congress Cataloging-in-Publication Data**

Weyland, Jack, 1940–
   On the run / Jack Weyland.
     p.   cm.
   Summary: Young Nathan, an elder in the Mormon Church, is aided in
his escape from murderous drug runners by a beautiful Lakota Sioux
girl who teaches him about her people as he shares the gospel with
her.
  ISBN 0-87579-891-8
  [1. Mormons—Fiction. 2. Mormon Church—Fiction. 3. Christian
life—Fiction. 4. Interpersonal relations—Fiction. 5. Dakota
Indians—Fiction. 6. Indians of North America—Fiction. 7. Drug
abuse—Fiction.]  I. Title.
PZ7.W538On    1995
[Fic]—dc20                               95-2956
                                                  CIP
                                                  AC

Printed in the United States of America

10  9  8   7   6   5   4   3   2   1

*This book is dedicated to the members of the
American Indian Science and Engineering Society
(AISES) at the South Dakota School of Mines
and Technology. I will always be grateful
for my association with you.*

# CHAPTER ONE

*Seattle, Washington: Thursday, June 9, 12:15 P.M.*

ELDER NATHAN WILLIAMS SHOOK HANDS with his mission president for the last time, waved to the elders who had come to see him off, then turned and gave his ticket to the agent at the gate. After two years, Nathan was going home.

Just before boarding the plane, Nathan glanced at his ticket. His seat assignment was 32A. He had requested a window seat so he could have one last look at Seattle, where he had spent his last six months working in the mission office. As fleet coordinator, his job had been to make sure all the mission cars were kept in good condition.

In Nathan's last interview, his mission president had commended him for being such a dedicated missionary. Nathan credited that mostly to his upbringing; helping his dad on the family farm had taught him how to work.

As he started down the aisle to his seat, he thought about how much he had changed while on his mission. Two years ago he had been so timid around strangers that it took all he had to ask the person next to him on the plane what he knew about the Mormon church. Now he felt at ease talking to just about anyone.

When he reached row 32, he noticed there was someone already in his seat. She had long, straight, brown hair even darker than his own. She looked to be either Indian or Hispanic. Her skin was the color of a Nestlé Crunch candy bar. The only time he got that dark was back home in Idaho after being outside all summer, but that was just on his face and arms and neck.

He had just spent two years trying not to think about girls, but he could hardly help noticing how beautiful she was, although her features seemed exaggerated—her cheekbones too high, her nose too pronounced, and her lips too full.

She appeared to be the kind of tourist that store owners dream about. She wore a Seattle Mariner baseball cap on her head and a Seattle SeaHawk T-shirt under her worn, brown leather jacket. In addition, she had a couple of large shopping bags stashed under the aisle seat.

"Excuse me," Nathan said, "but I think you're in my seat. I'm supposed to be in 32A. What seat do you have?"

She looked at her ticket. "You're right, I am in your seat. My seat is 32C."

He waited, but she didn't move. He cleared his throat.

"Would you mind sitting in my seat?" she asked. "If it's okay with you, I'd like to be by the window."

Nathan liked things to be done by the book. "If you wanted to be by the window, you should've said so when you got your ticket."

She tossed off his comment with a shrug of her shoulders. "I didn't think about it then. Besides, what difference does it make? There're not that many people sitting clear back here. I'm sure you can find yourself another window seat."

"I don't want to make a big deal out of this, but I'd really like to sit in my assigned seat. Why can't you move?"

"Look at all this stuff I've got—it'd take too long just to gather it all up."

"I'd be glad to help." Her expression told him that was not what she wanted. "I'm sorry to be such a pain," he continued, "but I really think people should sit in the seats they're assigned to. On the airline's computer they have you here and me there."

"Yeah, so?"

Nathan had to dig deep. "Well, if the plane crashes, if everyone is in their right seat, it'll make it easier to identify the bodies."

She put a hand to her mouth to hide a smile. "And you think we'll really care about that then?"

Nathan began to wonder if he'd been missionary fleet coordinator too long. "Well . . . "

"Just sit down, okay? People are waiting to get past you. We'll work something out. Maybe we can trade off who sits by the window."

Nathan knew he had every right to be in his assigned seat and that if he insisted he could get his way. But until he talked to his stake president back home, he was still a missionary, and it wasn't going to help his chances to tell her about the Church if she was mad at him. For that reason he gave up and sat in the aisle seat.

"Thanks," she said.

"No problem." But there was a problem. Because of her shopping bags he had no place to put his feet.

"Here, let me get that out of your way," she said.

There were two bags under his seat. "How about if I put them in the overhead?" he asked.

"Okay, that'd be great. Thanks."

He noticed some Indian beadwork in one of her bags. After stowing her things in the overhead, he sat down. "I hope you don't mind me asking, but are you Indian?"

"Yes, I'm Lakota Sioux. I'm from South Dakota."

"What are you doing in Seattle?"

"I've been here for a powwow."

"You came all this way to go to a powwow?" he asked.

"Yes. Why?"

"Well—I don't know—it just seems like a long way to go . . . you know . . . just for a powwow." As soon as he said it, he could tell by her expression that he'd made a mistake.

"Have you ever been to a powwow?" she asked.

"Well, not really."

"I didn't think so."

"I'm sorry for saying it the way I did. What I meant was— don't they have powwows in South Dakota?"

"Yeah, sure," she said. "I was invited to go to this one to

represent the Lakota people." She paused. "For the past year I've been Miss Indian America for South Dakota."

"Are you serious?" he asked. "That's great!"

"Thanks. It's been a good experience. Where are you from?"

"Rexburg, Idaho. Ever hear of it?"

"I don't think so," she said. "How far is it from Fort Hall Reservation?"

"It's about an hour's drive. How do you know about Fort Hall?"

"There's a big powwow there every year."

"I didn't know that. What town in South Dakota do you come from?"

"We don't live in a town. We're about twenty miles north of Kyle, on the Pine Ridge Indian Reservation. I live in the poorest county in the United States. Someday that's going to change though."

"What's going to make it change?" he asked.

"Education. The warriors of my people today are the ones who get a good education."

"Really? So, are you a warrior?"

"Yes, I am."

"What's your name?"

"Jessica Red Willow."

"It's really good to meet you. I'm Elder Williams." He flipped to the map in the back of the in-flight magazine. "Show me where you live, okay?"

She placed her finger on the map. "This is Rapid City where I go to college."

"What's the name of the college?"

"The South Dakota School of Mines and Technology." She moved her finger down and to the right. "This is about where Kyle is. When I'm not in school, like now, I live with my grand-mother way out in the hills north of Kyle. It's really kind of iso-lated. Our nearest neighbors are five miles away. We haul our own water and use a wood-burning stove for heating and cooking. It's rustic but I like it. Besides, there's some really nice country back where we live. Not too many people even know about it. And at night you can see a lot more stars than you can see in Seattle."

"No kidding. That's the way it is back on the farm where I come from."

"What brought you to Seattle? And why are you all dressed up?"

"For the past two years I've been a missionary for The Church of Jesus Christ of Latter-day Saints."

She looked at his name tag. "Is your first name really Elder?"

"No, 'elder' is what they call us while we're out here. We do this for two years and then we're done. In fact, I'm going home now—back to Rexburg. You should know about Rexburg because that's where the best potatoes in the world come from. That's what my dad does for a living—raises potatoes. I've been work-ing with him since I was a little kid. If you have any questions about potatoes, you'd better ask 'em now 'cause you'll probably never meet anyone who knows as much about potatoes as I do. And I know only about a tenth of what my dad knows."

She crinkled her nose. "What's there to know about a potato?"

"Quite a bit, actually. Like—did you know that when you store potatoes in a cellar they breathe?"

"I knew they had eyes, but where are their little noses?" When she laughed, she made very little sound.

Because it had been two years since Nathan had been alone with a girl, he felt a little guilty enjoying himself so much. He decided it was probably okay because with all the people on the plane he wasn't really alone with her.

"I'm serious. Here's something else. When you first put pota-toes in storage, they heal any wounds they might have gotten while they were being harvested."

"And do you go around from potato to potato, putting Band-Aids on their little bruises?" she teased.

"You don't believe me, do you." It was a statement rather than a question.

"Not a word."

"I'll tell you what—when I get home, I'll get my dad to write you a letter. He loves telling people about potatoes."

She glanced again at his name tag. "What's your real first name?"

"We don't go by first names on our mission."

"But you just told me your mission is over."

"It's not over till I talk to my stake president."

She looked confused. "Your steak president?"

"Yes."

"I see." She looked confused. "He's the president of a steak?"

"Yes, he is. The Rexburg East Stake."

"Really? Does he own a Sizzler?"

"Sizzler? No. Why do you ask?"

"You said he was a steak president."

Nathan stared at her for several seconds before he figured out what she was talking about. "It's not like a steak you eat. It's more like a stake you drive into the ground. You know, like for a tent."

She still had a puzzled expression on her face. "So this guy you have to see—he makes tent pegs? And he makes so many that people call him the stake president?"

"No, not really. The thing is, the word *stake* is symbolic. It has to do with stakes of Zion."

"So if a zion needs stakes, it must be some kind of a tent then. Right?"

"No. Zion is both a place and an attitude."

She shook her head and, with a good-natured grin, said, "Look, if you really don't want me to know, just say so."

"It's kind of hard to explain."

"You were a missionary for two years? What did you do?"

"I told people about our church."

"You've been doing this for two years, and you can't even tell me why you have to talk to a man in charge of stakes before I can call you by your first name?"

"He has to tell me I'm not a missionary anymore."

She gave him a playful smile. "I can save him the trouble. You're not a missionary anymore."

"I have to report to him in person. And then my two-year mission will be officially over."

"Two years, huh? There're not many guys your age who'd give up two years of their life to work for their church. By the way, how old are you?"

"Twenty-one."

"Me too," she said. "When were you born?"

"April 23."

"I was born in April too," she said. "Maybe that explains it."

"What?"

"When you sat down, I had the strangest feeling. I can't describe it. Maybe it's because we were born the same month."

"That's not it," he said.

"What is it then?"

"I have a message from God for you."

Nathan was puzzled by her reaction. At first her eyes opened wide, almost as if she were waiting for a message from God. But that was quickly replaced with skepticism. "Let's be honest here. Basically, all you want is for me to join your church—right?"

"Right now, all I want you to do is listen to what I have to say."

"Look, I guess you're sincere and everything—but the truth is, I really don't like to talk about religion."

"Why not?"

"Because people always end up arguing."

"That won't happen to us. Hey, you're the one who had the feeling when I sat down. Do you want me to tell you what it means or not?"

"There's no way you can know what it means," she said.

"Why not?"

"Don't take this wrong—the reason why you can't help me is because you're not Native American."

"What's that got to do with anything?"

"You'll just have to take my word for it—there's no way you can understand this."

"What are you going to do, go your whole life looking for a

message from God when I can give it you now, if you'll just listen?"

"I thought you said we weren't going to argue. Let's just back off on this, okay?"

"I could help you though," he said.

"Did you ever stop to think I might be able to help you?" she asked.

In two years, nobody had ever asked him that. And if anyone had, he would have dismissed the question; he had gone on a mission to teach, not to be taught. And yet, for one brief instant as they made eye contact, he had the feeling that in commitment and inner courage she was his equal.

"I'm sure I could learn a lot from you," he said. "But, even so, I do have a message from God for you." He paused, not sure if he should even say it. "You've been waiting a long time for it, haven't you?"

"Yes, but it won't come from you." To signal an end to the conversation, she picked up a magazine and turned to look out the window.

It was over. In a way Nathan was glad. He had spent two years keeping his distance from girls. He didn't want to spoil that by talking to a girl alone just before he reported to his stake president.

He could hardly wait to see his family again. Tomorrow morning, when he awakened, he'd have scripture study alone in his room and then he'd go out into the kitchen and his dad would be there and Nathan would spend the day with him in the fields.

Last year had not been a good year for raising potatoes. Erratic temperature changes had given some of the potatoes *hollow heart*. They looked good on the outside, but inside there might be one small part that was bad. Potatoes with hollow heart were, at best, second-rate.

That was last year. Every spring brought hope for the coming year's crop. But regardless of what the weather brought, they had to live with it. Farming was like trying to solve a new puzzle every year.

Working the land to produce a crop was never easy. Good

intentions were never enough. Either you did what was needed to coax the land to give you the production you needed to stay in business or else you didn't. Those who didn't soon gave it up to take up jobs in stores or leave town. Nathan's father usually did about as well as anybody.

Nathan's plans were simple. He'd finish college first and then go to work full-time on the farm. When his father retired, Nathan would run the place until his own sons replaced him. That was the way the land would pass from one generation to the next. Nathan realized it might not sound like much to some people, but it was all he wanted out of life.

Of course, he wouldn't always be single. He hoped that in a year or two he'd find the girl of his dreams and marry her in the Idaho Falls Temple.

He glanced at his watch. It was almost time for the flight to begin. He opened his scriptures and began to read.

▼ ▼ ▼

By the time Nathan was waiting for the plane to take off, his parents and fifteen-year-old sister, Kim, had been on the road for three hours. They had arranged to meet Nathan at the Salt Lake airport so that Nathan's two older brothers and their families could be there too. His brother John was an investment counselor in Salt Lake City, and his brother Andrew was in a graduate theater and film program at BYU.

Nathan's mother, Elaine Williams, was relieved to be on the road because it meant that she could finally relax. For the past month she had been busy getting everything ready for his return. She had prepared all his favorite foods and put them in the freezer. She had done a thorough cleaning of his room and put fresh sheets on his bed. She had even gone through a stack of pictures and organized them into a scrapbook. It had taken her days to do that, but she knew he'd be pleased. And she had made a large hand-lettered banner for her grandchildren to hold at the airport and arranged for as many family members as possible to be there when he stepped off the plane.

She had done something else she was sure that neither Nathan nor her husband, Boyd, would approve of. She had lent

Nathan's scrapbook to the girl she was hoping Nathan would come to appreciate as much as she did. Her name was Camille Stoddard. She came from a farm in western Idaho. Nathan hadn't even met her. Elaine had become acquainted with her while teaching private voice lessons to a few students from Ricks College. Camille was one of her students, a soprano with a voice so pure it seemed to come from heaven. With her short hair and captivating smile, Camille reminded Elaine of the actress Janine Turner on the television show *Northern Exposure.*

Because Camille had a brother on a mission, her family's finances were stretched to the limit. The only way she could afford to take private music lessons was by trading off services. And so once or twice a week she came to help Elaine around the house. Over the course of the past school year, they had done laundry, washed walls, canned fruit, wallpapered a room, and even sung duets together in church.

Elaine found herself fascinated by this girl who sang solos from the *Messiah* while vacuuming the living room or cleaning the oven. And even in jeans and a sweatshirt, she somehow managed to look elegant. The more time she spent with Camille, the more convinced Elaine became that Camille would be perfect for Nathan. Because Camille came from a farm, she'd fit in well with Nathan's plan to work with his dad after his mission. Running a family farm required that everyone get along, and she and Camille had made a great team.

Elaine was certain that Camille, if she were to marry Nathan, would also instill a love of good music in their children. She couldn't depend on Nathan for that; for some reason he had little appreciation for anything except country-western music.

Elaine knew she'd have to be careful in trying to get Nathan and Camille together. When Nathan was in high school, she had once told him how much she admired one of the girls in the ward. After that he made it a point to avoid the girl.

Even Camille had made it clear she didn't appreciate parents who tried to pick their children's mates. She had complained once about how her mother had tried to line her up with a returned missionary. Camille made it sound as if her mother had tried to sell her into slavery.

Camille was everything Elaine wanted for her son and for the grandchildren who would come. She was refined, she loved music, she played the piano and sang, and she wasn't afraid to work. She had been raised in a good LDS farm family.

*But one thing at a time. First, let's get Nathan home,* she thought, *and then I'll worry about introducing him to Camille.*

She was surprised by how excited she was about Nathan's return. Having already sent two other sons on missions, she thought she would have been a hardened veteran. But it didn't work that way; she had missed Nathan a great deal. He was her youngest son, her baby, and, unlike John and Andrew, he had never quit giving her hugs—even when he was in high school.

In the last few weeks she had spent many hours in Nathan's room. She rationalized she was getting it ready for his return, but sometimes she just sat on his bed and looked at his pictures and remembered his childhood.

And now the day she had waited for so long had finally come. Nathan was coming home.

▼ ▼ ▼

Boyd Williams's response to deep feelings was often silence. Today he had been especially silent because his son Nathan was coming home from his mission.

*I've been through this two times before,* he thought. *So why is it so different this time?* Boyd knew the answer—Nathan was the only one of his three sons who wanted to become a farmer like him.

Boyd couldn't explain how much his land meant to him. It wasn't just so many acres here and so many there. It was a living entity, an extension of his family. His entire past, present, and future were tied up in his farm. He had grown up working along-side his father on some of the same land that he and Nathan had worked together.

Because Boyd believed in teaching children how to work, all his sons had gotten an early start. He had taught each boy to drive a tractor when he was ten years old. By the time John and

Andrew were in high school, though, they were tired of the long hours. John got a job working in a clothing store in Rexburg, and Andrew tried out for every play he could. Nathan was the only one who stayed with his dad all through high school and worked hard every day during the summer and fall without complaining.

With Nathan gone, Boyd had gotten by with part-time, hired help, but it was not the same. Most people he hired took no pleasure in their work. They did the minimum and that was all. Boyd had no patience with people like that. Working with Nathan wasn't just a matter of getting chores done right the first time. It was teaching his son all he knew and enjoying the feeling they shared for the land. The land was a legacy that must be preserved, and Nathan would be the one to carry that legacy into the next generation.

Nathan, his pride and joy, the son who was like him in so many ways, was finally coming home.

▼ ▼ ▼

Nathan's fifteen-year-old sister, Kim, was also glad Nathan was coming home, even though it meant she would have to give up his CD player, his VCR, and what was left of his TV. She wanted him home because with him gone, their house seemed like a retirement village.

She remembered Nathan's freshman year at Ricks. He was bringing people home all the time. The house was full of laughter and jokes and pizza. Their parents never seemed to mind something like that when Nathan did it. But let her bring some of her friends home after a dance at school, and you'd think they were having a wild party with drinking and everything, when all they were doing was watching a movie and eating popcorn.

Her parents had become set in their ways. She hoped Nathan would turn all that around once he got home. Then maybe they'd loosen up a little and give her some freedom too. It wasn't that she was asking for a lot. She only wanted to be able to stay out later on weekends and to be able to have sleepovers with her friends from school. And she wanted her own car. Nathan had had his own pickup by the time he was a senior; he had paid for it himself from money he earned on the farm.

There was another reason she was anxious to see Nathan
again. She wanted him to see her. She had become almost a
woman since he'd been gone. She looked a lot older than she was,
and when she was with older boys who weren't from Rexburg,
she often lied about her age and they believed her.

She knew what Nathan would say about how she had grown
up, but she wanted to hear it anyway. She was excited to have her
big brother come home.

▼ ▼ ▼

Just before the plane's scheduled departure time, one more
passenger entered the plane. On his way down the aisle he paused
at the row where Nathan and Jessica were sitting. "Excuse me,"
he said. "Looks like I'm in the middle."

Nathan stood up to let him get to his seat. The man appeared
to be in his midforties. He smelled of cigarette smoke and looked
as if he'd slept a couple of days in his clothes—a brown tweed
sportcoat, wrinkled white shirt with loosened tie, and brown
pants. His head was bald on top, but his hair was long around the
sides.

Nathan was disappointed to have this stranger sit down
between him and Jessica. Even if they hadn't agreed on everything, he had enjoyed talking to her.

The newcomer settled into his seat. He glanced nervously at
his watch and then up the aisle. "We should be pulling away from
the gate now," he said, nervously drumming his fingers on the arm
rest.

The plane's captain announced they were waiting for passengers from another flight.

"Great, that's all I need," the man muttered.

"Is anything wrong?" Nathan asked.

"No, everything's fine and dandy," he grumbled.

Nathan stuck out his hand. "I'm Elder Williams."

The man ignored him. His eyes were fixed forward. "Let's
go, let's go . . . "

"Kind of in a hurry, huh?" Nathan asked.

"You could say that."

Nathan started reading again. Less than a minute later he was interrupted by the man next to him swearing under his breath. Nathan looked up and noticed another passenger making his way slowly down the aisle. He seemed to be looking for someone. He was wearing a blue blazer and what looked to be a very expensive silk tie.

The man in the middle seat turned to Nathan. "Listen to me. We don't have much time." He pulled a computer disk from his jacket pocket and handed it to Nathan. "My name is Gibbs," he said softly. "I'm with the FBI. If anything happens to me, deliver this to Senator Michael Montgomery from the state of Washington. He'll know what to do with it. Don't give it to anyone else. And whatever you do, don't contact the police or the FBI. People's lives depend on this."

At first Nathan thought it was a joke, but as he looked at Gibbs's expression, there could be no doubting his seriousness. Nathan glanced at the disk. "What's on this that makes it so important?"

"There's no time to explain that now. Listen, there's no way I'm going to be allowed to take this flight. If I somehow get out of here alive, get off the plane and meet me at the Pike Place Fish Market this afternoon. You can give me back the disk and then be on your way again on a later flight."

Nathan noticed that Jessica was listening intently to Gibbs.

"How about if I just mail it to you? I really don't want to miss this flight. My whole family is meeting me in Salt Lake City."

Gibbs gripped Nathan's arm. "Do what I say. There's another plane leaving for Salt Lake City in a couple of hours. I'll buy your ticket. Now put that disk away so he doesn't see it."

Nathan did as he was told. "But why? What's going on?"

"See that man coming this way? His name's Steiger. He's going to try to kill me."

A moment later Steiger stopped at their row. He kept his right hand in his right-side suit pocket. He nodded to Gibbs, then said to Nathan and Jessica, "Excuse me, but I wonder if I could talk to my friend here. Would you two mind moving? It'll just be for a minute."

They didn't have to be asked twice. Near the back of the

plane, where they were sitting, there were several empty seats. Nathan sat down in a vacant aisle seat at 33C, one row behind where he'd been. Jessica sat in 31D, across the aisle and one row in front of where she'd been.

Steiger sat down next to Gibbs. "Dave, we've been worried about you," he said warmly. "When you didn't show up for work this morning, and you didn't answer our phone calls, we were concerned that something might have happened to you."

"Nothing's wrong. I just thought I'd take a few days off," Gibbs said.

Nathan set his scriptures on the tray table in front of him and leaned forward. Instead of reading, he strained to pick up the conversation in the row ahead. He glanced at Jessica. She had a magazine open, but he could tell she was listening too. The only other person close enough to hear Gibbs and Steiger was a young woman in the row ahead of them, but she had earphones on and was listening to her tape player, her shoulders moving to the beat of the music.

There was nothing threatening in Steiger's manner, and yet Nathan had the feeling he was like a robot who appeared to be human but was actually without feelings and somehow very dangerous.

"You're going to Washington, D.C., aren't you," Steiger said.

"How did you find that out?" Gibbs asked.

"You didn't make it easy for me, that's for sure. It was almost as though you didn't want anyone to know your plans."

"You always were too suspicious. I just decided I needed a little break, that's all."

"That's what I thought," Steiger said pleasantly. "Just a few days visiting our nation's capital, right?"

"That's right."

Steiger reached up to check if his tie was still in place. "I don't have a problem with that. All of us could stand to be more patriotic. But you know how Donovan is—I swear he worries enough for five or six people put together. When you didn't show up this morning, he started to check around. Well, you can imagine his surprise when he found out that at two o'clock this morning, someone made two copies of certain confidential files from his computer. Isn't it strange that someone would be working that late? You're the only one in the office who works that hard—day in, day out—just like the Energizer Bunny."

"It wasn't me."

"You know what? That's exactly what I told Donovan. But he still wants to talk to you. In fact, he's waiting inside the terminal. I'll take you to him and you can tell him all about your vacation plans. I'm sure everything will turn out just fine. I mean, after all, Donovan is as patriotic as they come. So let's go see him, shall we?"

"I'm not going with you," Gibbs declared.

"You're not?"

"No."

"I thought we were friends," Steiger said.

"Not really. We just work together."

Steiger sighed and lowered his voice. "Well, it's up to you, of course, but if you won't come with me, then I'll have to kill you. I have a gun pointed at you now, but you probably knew that."

"If you're going to kill me, do it now," Gibbs said.

"Sitting here, next to you? Think of the mess—this is a new tie."

"If you kill me here, maybe people will start asking questions."

"Dave, Dave, Dave, you always underestimate me. Do you really think I'd come in here without some kind of backup?"

"What's your backup?" Gibbs asked.

"I know something you don't know—about your twelve-year-old daughter."

"I made sure she'd be safe," Gibbs said.

"Yeah, sure—just like you took care of getting on this plane without me finding you. We've got your daughter, Dave."

"You're lying."

"I talked to her just before coming to the airport. It was really very touching. She had tears in her eyes. She told me she wants to go home. Actually, though, Donovan is thinking of sending her to Colombia. They do such a nice job there with the people we send them."

Gibbs's shoulders slumped. "What do you want?"

"Not much, actually. Donovan wants to talk to you inside the terminal, and he wants the two disks you copied his files on."

"What about my daughter?"

"We don't have anything personal against her. Just give us what we want, and we'll let her go. We'll work out any arrangements you want to make sure she gets out unharmed."

"All right, you win. When I saw you coming, I gave one of the disks to the guy who was sitting next to me."

"The one who looks like a Boy Scout in a blue suit?" Steiger asked.

"Yeah."

"So, is he your little helper these days?"

"No, just somebody I met on the plane."

"Well, if that's what you say, it must be true because you'd never lie to me, would you? What about the other disk?"

"You can have it once I know my daughter is safe."

"Fair enough. Before I turn around to talk to your friend, why don't you give me your gun?"

Gibbs slowly retrieved a gun from inside his jacket and handed it to Steiger.

"Thanks." Tucking Gibbs's weapon into his belt, Steiger stood up and turned to talk to Nathan. "Excuse me. This man gave you a computer disk a few minutes ago. Now he'd like you to give it to me."

"Who are you?"

"I'm with the FBI, and if you don't want to be arrested for obstructing justice, I suggest you give me the disk immediately."

"If you work for the FBI, how about showing me your badge?" Nathan asked.

Steiger displayed his badge. Nathan studied it carefully.

"Any questions?" Steiger asked.

"Since when does the FBI kidnap twelve-year-old girls?"

"That does it. Sir, you're under arrest. By the time I'm done with you, you'll spend the next five years in federal prison."

Gibbs turned around. "It's okay—give him the disk."

As Nathan reached into his inside suit pocket, Steiger tensed up, assuming he might be going for a weapon. "Slowly, slowly. What's that bulge in your suit pocket?"

"Missionary pamphlets."

Gibbs, seeing Steiger preoccupied with Nathan, reached carefully for another pistol he had in an ankle holster. He removed the gun and, springing up, slammed Steiger in the side of the head with it. Steiger slumped down, unconscious.

The young woman in 31A continued to listen to her music, but an older couple in row 34 had watched what happened. Gibbs went back to them and flashed his badge. To them and anyone else who might have seen what had happened, he said, "I'm an undercover agent with the FBI. This man just tried to sell me a large shipment of drugs. I need to go now and confiscate the drugs and arrest the others involved in the operation. Other agents are on their way to arrest the man I just knocked out."

Gibbs handcuffed Steiger's arm to the tray table and retrieved his own weapon from Steiger's belt, then came to Nathan. He leaned down and spoke fast and low. "There're others like this guy in the terminal. I'm getting out of here before they come in to get me. If you want to stay alive, you'd better come with me."

"Why? I haven't done anything wrong."

"You helped me—that's all the reason they'll need. I'll explain it all once we get to safety. C'mon, c'mon, we don't have all day!"

Nathan scrambled to his feet. Jessica turned and looked at him.

"Get his gun," Gibbs said to Nathan. "You might need it."

Nathan's mouth dropped open. "Why?"

"In case people start shooting at us, that's why," Gibbs said sarcastically.

Nathan looked at Gibbs with a bewildered expression.

"Never mind, I'll get it." Gibbs reached into Steiger's right, front suit pocket and grabbed the unconscious man's gun. "Okay, let's go."

Jessica touched Nathan's arm as he was leaving. "If you need any help, I'll meet you later today at that fish market Gibbs talked about. What was it, the Pike Place Fish Market?"

"You'll miss your flight."

"I can always catch a later flight."

"Move it! Move it!" Gibbs said to Nathan. "Here, take Steiger's gun."

Gibbs handed it to him. The pistol was heavy and felt foreign in his hand. As he followed Gibbs up the aisle, he wondered if it had a safety or if all he had to do was pull the trigger. He raised it to get a closer look at it.

A boy near the front of the plane saw him. "Look, Mommy, there's a missionary, and he's got a gun."

Nathan ripped his name tag off and stuffed it along with the gun into his suit pocket.

# CHAPTER TWO

*Seattle: 12:52 P.M.*

INSTEAD OF GOING UP THE RAMP INTO THE TERMINAL, Gibbs and
Nathan ran down the service stairs and across the tarmac to the
nearest door of the terminal and then through one service area
after another. Finally they passed down a long, narrow hallway
that led to the airport parking ramp.

"That's my van over there," Gibbs said, gasping for breath.
He pointed to a rust-covered, beat-up van with "Ace Plumbing
Supply and Repair" painted on the side.

The inside of the van consisted of a shell stuffed with plumbing parts, but inside that, there was a small enclosed area, impossible to be seen from the outside. This space was filled with electronic instruments. A tired-looking blonde in her late thirties
looked up as they entered. She was listening to communications
between the tower and pilots of planes about to take off.

"What happened? Everything was fine and then all of a sudden your pilot was calling for airport security and an ambulance."
Her voice was low and gravelly.

"Steiger found me on the plane. I got lucky and ended up
knocking him out with my gun."

The woman looked at Nathan. "Who's he?" she asked.

"Just some poor guy who happened to be at the wrong place
at the wrong time."

The three of them sat on tiny stools in a cramped plywood

shell lit by a single bulb. Nathan had the feeling that none of this was really happening, that it was all just a dream.

"I'm Rita," the woman said.

"Hi. I'm Elder Williams."

"Give me the disk," Gibbs said.

Nathan handed it to him. Gibbs put it in his shirt pocket and then grabbed a phone.

"What are you doing?" Rita asked.

"Calling Shirley."

"Who's Shirley?" Nathan asked.

"His ex-wife," Rita said. "Dave and I are married now."

Rita took it upon herself to entertain Nathan while Gibbs made his call. "I'm dying for a cigarette, but we can't smoke when we're in here because the smoke would give us away. So we chew gum. Want some?"

Nathan reached for a stick of gum. "Thanks." He tried to listen to two conversations at the same time—to Gibbs, who was talking to his ex-wife to find out if their daughter was safe, and to Rita, who was saying how wrong she thought it was for teachers not to let kids chew gum in school.

Gibbs finally hung up. "My daughter's okay. Steiger was trying to con me."

"You want to tell me what this is all about?" Nathan asked.

Gibbs looked at him and asked, "You ever wonder why the price of cocaine is so low in this country?"

Nathan felt like he'd been suddenly transported to another planet. "I didn't know the price was low."

"Cheap as a trip to McDonald's," Rita said.

"Why?"

"Because there's so much of the stuff coming in," Gibbs said. "Millions of dollars' worth enters Seattle every month. You ever wonder why it keeps coming in, month after month? Because people in high places are paid to look the other way."

"Donovan, Donovan, he's our man. If he can't be bought off, nobody can," Rita chanted, then laughed hoarsely.

"Who's Donovan?" Nathan asked.

Gibbs continued. "Jack Donovan is the FBI agent in charge

of the Seattle area. The drug syndicate is paying him big bucks. Steiger, the guy who busted up our travel plans, works for him."

"You *both* work for the FBI?" Nathan asked.

Gibbs nodded. "That's why we both had guns on the plane. All we had to do was flash our badges to get through security."

"Tell him how you got into this," Rita said.

"I was assigned to work in the Seattle office last year."

"One of the few honest agents Donovan had," Rita added.

"Not true, most are honest," Gibbs said. "It's just the few nearest Donovan that are bad. Three months ago I began to realize something was wrong. I started poking around. It didn't take long to discover what was happening. At first I didn't know how many agents were involved. I didn't know who I could trust, so I got in touch with Senator Michael Montgomery. He said he'd heard that Donovan was on the take. He cleared it through the head of the FBI to have me see what I could find out. Because we didn't know how high the corruption went, the deal was that I'd report directly to Montgomery and then he'd take it to the director of the FBI. Last night I went into Donovan's office and copied enough files to send him to jail for the rest of his life. I was on my way to see Senator Montgomery in Washington, D.C., when Steiger found me."

"What are you going to do now?" Nathan asked.

"Donovan knows what files I've copied, so he'll be going back and covering his tracks. I've got to find some people who will agree to testify about what's going on. It'll probably take a couple of weeks. If you want to stay alive, you'll have to hide out until then."

"Look, I really don't want to get involved in this. I just want to go home."

"You can't go home for a while. If you do, you'll not only set yourself up to be killed but you'll also put your family in danger. These are vicious people, and they don't care who they hurt."

"But I don't know anything."

"Look at it from Steiger's point of view. When he came onto the plane, you were sitting next to me. You also turn out to be the one holding the disk. He'll find out that you and I left the plane together. Not only that, but when you left you were carrying his gun. As far as Steiger and Donovan are concerned, that adds up to the fact that you and I were working together. They want me dead and out of the way, and they'll need to kill you too if they want to keep things neat and tidy. And even if it's a mistake to kill you, it's not going to keep 'em up at night. So if you want to stay alive, you've got to run."

"You'd better listen to him," Rita said. "He knows what he's talking about. You're gonna have to be on the run for a while."

"But I haven't been home in two years."

"You'll be home soon enough," Gibbs said. "Give me two weeks. By then I'll be able to move against Donovan and his men. Just two weeks."

"Let me go home and be with my family for a couple of days first," Nathan asked.

Rita started laughing. "Oh, my gosh, where did you get this guy anyway? What does he think—that he can call time-out?"

"Once you see your family," Gibbs explained, "you put them in jeopardy also, and Steiger will add them to his list of people to kill. Is that what you want?"

Nathan sighed. "No. But how can I hide out? Where will I go? I don't even have any money."

From a small black bag Gibbs pulled out a stack of money with a big rubber band around it. The money was separated with paper clips into bundles of ten one-hundred-dollar bills each. Gibbs counted out ten bundles and handed them to Nathan. "Here's ten thousand dollars. That ought to be enough to get you by for a couple of weeks."

Nathan ran his finger over the money. It was more than he had ever before seen in his life. "I don't need this much. I was just thinking maybe a bus ticket and some money for groceries."

"You never know," Gibbs said. "Hiding out can be expensive. And you have to use cash. You can't use credit cards or ATM machines because that'll give you away."

"Quiet, someone's coming!" Rita warned.

Gibbs turned off the overhead light. They sat in silence and total darkness, listening to nearby voices. Gibbs picked up his gun just in case. Nathan reached for his gun too, although he didn't know what he'd do if he ever had to use it. He realized he didn't even know what kind of a gun it was. He felt like his life was spinning out of control, and he tried to go over once again how he had gotten involved in this. *I'm trying to go home after my mission, and a man asks me to hold something for him for a few minutes,* he thought. *Then all of a sudden, I've got a gun and I'm waiting to see if I end up having to use it in order to stay alive.*

They heard the sound of a car door being slammed, and then the car next to them started up. Soon it was quiet again. Rita poked her head out of the back door of the van to make sure it was safe. "They've gone." She closed the door, locked it in place, and turned on the light again so they could see.

When the light went on, the first thing Nathan saw was the hundred-dollar bills stacked neatly in ten rows. "You don't even know me, so why are you giving me all this money?"

"It's worth it to me to keep you alive so you can testify at Steiger's trial. Use the money to go into hiding for the next two weeks. If you have any left over, turn it in then. Find a place to go where nobody would ever think to look for you. And wherever it is, don't tell me—in case they find me."

Gibbs looked at the calendar on his watch. "Let's see, today is June ninth. We need to work out a signal so you'll know when it's safe to come out of hiding. Two weeks from now is the twenty-third. If everything goes according to schedule, in the Sunday paper for . . . let's see, how about the twenty-sixth?—I'll place an ad under 'Pets for Sale.' The ad will read 'Golden retriever puppies. Must sell. Only one left. Call after five or weekends.' There'll be a fake phone number to call. You got that?"

"Yeah, sure. What paper will the ad be in?"

"That's up to you. Do you have any idea what general area you might end up in?"

Nathan thought about it. "I've got an uncle who has a hunting cabin in Colorado. It's empty this time of year. I might go there."

"Okay, how about if I put the ad in the *Denver Post*?"

"Okay."

Gibbs continued his instructions. "If the ad says there's one puppy left, that means you're free to head home. If the ad says that there's two, then that means you'll need to wait and then check again the next week."

"Don't I have any choice in this?"

"Yeah, you've got a choice. Either you do exactly what I tell you and stay alive, or else you do it your way and get yourself and maybe your family killed. Those are your only choices. Look, kid, I'm sorry you got involved in this, but that's the way it is. Maybe it's time you find out that life isn't always fair."

Nathan still wasn't satisfied. "First you say two weeks, and now you're talking like it might go three weeks or even more. Exactly how long is it going to take?"

Gibbs grabbed the ten thousand dollars and flung it at the wall, then slammed his fist on the floor. "That's it! Get out of here! Go get your head blown off—see if I care!"

"I just asked a question," Nathan said, trying to defend himself.

"Yeah, but your question tells me you don't have the slightest idea how much trouble you're in. Let me tell you something—I wouldn't bet ten dollars that you're going to be alive tomorrow at this time. So don't go saying that if I don't wrap this up in exactly two weeks, it'll be inconvenient for you. You want to know what's inconvenient? Getting your head blown off!"

"Would you just listen to me for once?" Nathan said. "The reason I'm so anxious to get home is because I've just finished serving a mission for my church, and I haven't been home for two years! When the plane lands in Salt Lake City, my whole family will be waiting for me. When I don't show up, they'll eventually report it to the police."

"Good, I hope they do," Gibbs said. "Maybe that'll put some pressure on Donovan."

"But what about my family? They won't know what happened to me."

"Okay, they'll be upset," Gibbs said. "But at least they'll be alive. Besides, you'll be home soon enough. They've waited two years. What's another few weeks?"

Rita tried to smooth things over. "But really, Dave, most likely it'll be just a couple of weeks, right?"

Gibbs nodded. "Yeah, most likely." He looked over at Nathan. "Can we continue now?"

"All right," Nathan said.

Gibbs went on. "If there's no ad in the *Denver Post,* or if you find out something's happened to me, go to Washington, D.C., find Senator Montgomery, and give him the disk and tell him everything you know. You got that? He's our only hope. Don't trust anyone but him."

"Would it be all right if I phoned my family?"

"No, you can't call. The minute you do, Donovan will track the call and have both you and your family killed. Don't call them. Don't call anyone."

"You just called your wife."

"Ex-wife," Rita put in. "He used a special phone and a coded signal."

"How about if I write a letter?"

Gibbs shook his head impatiently. "I'm just not getting through to you, am I. Let's try it one more time. If you communicate *anything* to your family, Steiger will assume you've told 'em everything. And someday he'll knock on the door and blow them away."

"But they'll be at the airport waiting for me."

Gibbs nodded. "I understand that. I'm sorry. It's a tough break for you. But that's the way it is."

"If I take your money and the disk, then I really will be working for you, and Donovan will be justified in having me killed."

Gibbs shrugged his shoulders. "What's the difference? Donovan's going to send Steiger to kill you anyway. So what have you got to lose by helping me out?"

Nathan sighed, took the disk from Gibbs, gathered up the money, and put it in his suit pocket.

"I need to tell you a few things about the disk," Gibbs continued. "First of all, it's not a common system, so most computers won't read it. Second, the information detailing Donovan's operation is nested. This is how it works: Say you pull up one of the files and what you see is a letter from Donovan to his office staff telling them not to use so many paper clips. You have to go to one of the words in the letter, and hit two code keys simultaneously—say the Control and Alternate keys—and then that lets you into the second file. And another thing, if you put the disk in an ordinary PC, all the information on the disk will self-destruct."

"What are you trying to say?" Rita asked.

Gibbs's glare bore into Nathan. "Don't mess with my disk."

Nathan nodded. "All right."

Gibbs continued. "You'll have to be real careful. Donovan and Steiger are good at finding people. You give them one tiny lead, you make one long-distance phone call to your folks, you use a credit card one time, you write even one letter home, and I promise that Steiger'll be at your door the next day. Your first priority right now is to stay alive. Everything else comes in a distant second."

"Are you two done now?" Rita asked.

"Yeah, I think so," Gibbs said.

"I can drive if you want, Sweetie," she said.

"That'd be great," Gibbs said. He turned to Nathan. "Where do you want us to drop you off?"

Nathan remembered Jessica's offer to help him. "The Pike Place Fish Market."

"No problem."

While Rita drove, Nathan and Gibbs stayed in the enclosure. Gibbs looked carefully at Nathan and said, "You will get out of those duds, won't you? With the suit on, you might as well be walking around with a bull's-eye on your chest."

"Okay. Anything else?"

"How are you going to get out of town?"

"I don't know. Take a bus, I guess."

"Forget it. They'll be watching the bus depots."

"I guess with this money I could buy a used car."

"By the end of business today, Steiger will have called every car dealer and asked if a guy matching your description has bought a car. When he finds out where you bought it, he'll have the number of your temporary plates, too. He can have the highway patrol track you wherever you go. The best thing, if you're going to buy a car, is to have someone else buy it for you."

"I'm not going to put anybody else in danger."

Gibbs shrugged his shoulders. "Then as soon as you get out of town, find a car that's not going anywhere for a long time and switch plates."

Half an hour later, Rita called out, "We're here."

Nathan crawled out of the enclosure. "Well," he said. He really didn't know what to say. Somehow "Have a nice day" didn't seem appropriate.

"You got your money, honey?" Rita asked.

Nathan nodded.

"You got the disk?" she asked.

He nodded.

She looked at him with what for her might have been an expression of tenderness. "Well, go out there and get lost." She looked sad as she drove away.

Outside now for the first time, Nathan wondered with each step if Steiger was somewhere up on a hill or in a car and had him in the telescopic sight of his gun.

This was a strange new world he had just entered.

▼ ▼ ▼

*2:15 P.M.*

Of all the places to arrange a meeting, the Pike Place Fish Market would have been Nathan's last choice. He didn't like to eat fish; in fact, he didn't even like to be around them. The fish market was no place to order a soft drink and sit around and watch the seagulls near the bay, but it was entertaining. When a customer decided on a particular fish, the salesman yelled the order to a clerk, who then flung it through the air to the counter, where it was caught, filleted, and wrapped.

Nathan stayed around long enough to make sure Jessica wasn't there and then walked around. It was a beautiful, sunny day in Seattle, but it felt strange to still be there without a companion, when he should have been well on his way home. If he hadn't been a hunted man, he'd have walked down to Waterfront

Park and taken in the view. But now, for the first time in his life, he didn't feel safe.

As he walked around, he found a store specializing in outdoor clothing for tourists who wanted to look like either a lumberjack or a fisherman. He went in and bought a pair of designer jeans, some hiking boots, a brown plaid wool shirt, a hooded sweatshirt, a light jacket, and a daypack.

"That will be two hundred seventy-nine dollars," the clerk said.

Nathan didn't want to show the clerk his stack of money. "Can I pay you after I change?" he asked.

"Sure, no problem."

In the dressing room Nathan went through all the pockets in his suit. He put his suit in the bag the clerk had given him to hold the things he'd just bought. The suit was nearly worn-out and threadbare and he decided to throw it away in the nearest garbage can outside the building. He didn't have the heart to throw away his name tag, though. He put it in the bottom of his daypack. He decided he'd keep the computer disk in his shirt pocket. He palmed three one-hundred-dollar bills to pay for what he'd bought and placed seven other bills from the first pack of money in his wallet; the rest he tucked into his daypack.

Three o'clock passed, but Jessica didn't come. He moved to a coffee shop and waited. *There's no reason to expect she'll come,* he thought. *Why should she miss her plane for someone she's just barely met?*

He decided to wait until five o'clock and then leave. More than anything, he wanted to get out of town. He'd told Gibbs he might go to his uncle's cabin. The only problem was that he had only been there once, and that was when he was twelve. He wasn't really sure where it was.

For the past two years, whenever he needed advice, he always had gone to his mission president. He thought of going to him about this too. But he knew what Gibbs would say—that if he did, and Steiger found out, then his mission president would become a target. This reminded him of a childhood game in which one person is Poison and everybody he touches becomes Poison too. *I'm Poison now,* he thought.

At three forty-five he saw a cab pull up to the fish market and Jessica get out. By the time he got to her, she was inside the market.

"Thanks for coming," he said, taking her arm. "Let's get out of here."

He took her to the coffee shop, where they ordered peppermint tea because it was recommended by their waiter.

"Sorry it took so long," she said. "First the police came and then an ambulance. They wanted to take Steiger to the hospital, but he wouldn't go. And then this other guy showed up. He said his name was Donovan and that he was with the FBI. He said a few words to the cops, and they all disappeared. You should see this guy. He looks like a diplomat, not a cop—dark hair peppered with gray, a voice that sounds like he's got his head in a barrel. The first thing they did was empty the plane and search it, and then they started going through everybody's luggage. And then Donovan interviewed everybody. He spent a lot of time with me because someone had noticed you and me together. He wanted to know all about you."

"What did you tell him?"

"Not much. I played into his racist attitudes. He didn't expect much from me, and that's what he got. I didn't see anything, I didn't hear anything, I really don't know what's going on. I'm pretty sure he bought it. Oh, one other thing, he confiscated your suitcase. Just before he let us go, he went into this big explanation that for months they've been working on an undercover operation to try to put the leaders of a drug-dealing empire behind bars. He said any publicity about what happened today would destroy years of work and endanger the undercover agents. He got everybody to sign a statement they won't talk to anyone about what happened. So the police aren't looking for you or Gibbs. Everybody's home free. But why?"

"Donovan doesn't want Gibbs or me arrested because we might talk to the wrong people," Nathan said. "How'd you get here?"

"Donovan impounded the plane but then told us the airline

had managed to book everybody on the four-thirty flight. As soon as they let us go, I came here. I don't even know where my luggage is, probably on its way to Salt Lake City."

Nathan glanced to his left and noticed four guys at a nearby table staring at them. His first fear was that they were after him, but then he realized it was Jessica they were interested in.

"What'd you find out?" she asked.

"I don't know for sure, but I think Gibbs is one of the good guys. He's about to nail Donovan. He told me that Donovan is being paid a lot of money to keep drugs coming in."

"When does Gibbs think he'll be able to arrest Donovan?" she asked.

"In a couple of weeks. He has a few loose ends to tie up."

"What are you going to do till then?" Jessica asked.

"Try to keep from getting killed."

"Steiger will be looking for you too, won't he?"

"That's what Gibbs says. You won't believe what he gave me."

"What?" she asked.

"Ten thousand dollars," he said softly.

"Wow! What for?"

"To stay on the run."

"That's a lot of money."

"That's what I told him. He said it's better to have too much than not enough."

"So you're going to just keep moving?"

"I guess so. I've thought about buying a car."

She didn't say anything for a long time and then asked, "You want to stay with me? I can't offer you much, because my grandmother's place is really small. She's getting kind of old and gets confused real easily these days, so it'd probably be better if she didn't even know you were around. But you could camp out in the hills above our place. Nobody ever goes there, and I could bring you food and water at night. The reservation is a great place to hide."

"If Steiger finds you and me together, he'll kill you too. Why risk your life for someone you hardly even know?"

"Because . . . " She stopped. It was the same sequence of reactions he'd noticed earlier—sincerity and idealism followed by cynicism. "You've got plenty of money. For a thousand dollars, I'll help you hide out at my place."

"You're willing to risk your life for a thousand dollars?"

"I'm not worried. Once I get you home, you'll be safe. And for me it'll be an easy way to pick up some extra money. I can always use a few extra dollars."

Because she didn't strike him as the materialistic type, he found it hard to believe she'd help him just for the money. For a moment he wondered if she was working for Steiger and if Steiger had sent her to kill him. He needed to know what to do, but he wasn't well-equipped to deal with things like this. For the past two years he had learned to trust his feelings more than logic or reason. He would have to rely on his feelings for this too.

"Can I trust you?" he asked.

She made eye contact with him. "Yeah, you can."

He believed she was telling the truth. "All right. Thanks. Maybe we should leave now. You want to pick up some nice cod while we're here?"

"No. But if we're going to be partners, there is something I need to know."

"What?"

"What should I call you?"

"Huh?"

"What's your name? Or should I call you *Elder Williams*?"

Nathan reflected for a moment. It didn't look as if he was going to get released right away. Still, revealing his first name to this pretty young woman seemed to be breaking mission rules. But she was right. If they were going to be on the run together, she had to call him something.

"It's Nathan," he said, wincing slightly.

She reached out her hand and he responded by giving her a missionary handshake.

"Well, Nathan, we'd better get going. We've got a long drive ahead of us."

*Yes, and plenty of reasons to be terrified, too,* Nathan thought.

# CHAPTER THREE

As their taxicab pulled away, Nathan kept looking back to make sure they weren't being followed.

"Where to?" the taxi driver asked.

"Just someplace where we can buy a used car," Nathan said.

From the interstate, he watched as they passed two car lots. "Where are you taking us?" he asked the cab driver.

"I know a place where you can get a good deal. It's where I get all my cars."

"I don't care about getting a good deal," Nathan complained.

"He's just kidding," Jessica said, leaning forward with a big smile. "We have to watch our pennies just like everybody else." She leaned against Nathan and whispered in his ear, "You go telling people you don't care if you get a good deal, and they're going to remember that, so if Steiger comes around asking questions, they'll remember you, and he'll be able to track us down. Is that what you want?"

Nathan had just spent two years at arm's length, and now Jessica was leaning against him and whispering in his ear. He cleared his throat. "You're right. Sorry. Oh, just one thing, don't get so close to me, okay? Arm's length is close enough."

She mumbled something and moved as far away as she could.

"If you have something to say, say it loud enough so I can hear it," Nathan said.

"You wouldn't like what I said."

The cab driver glanced in his rearview mirror at them. Nathan leaned forward. "My wife and I care about getting a good deal like everybody else."

"You two don't get along very well, do you," the cab driver observed.

Nathan nodded. "I'm hoping it'll get better."

The driver spoke man to man. "I guess you two came from the opposite sides of the tracks, huh?"

"Something like that," Nathan said.

A few minutes later they pulled into a used-car lot. Nathan paid the driver, got out, and held the door for Jessica. She got out and the taxi pulled away. She looked up at the large sign: Big Chief Auto Sales. A caricature of an Indian chief looked stoically down at them.

"We can't stay here," she said.

"I don't see we have much choice."

"We have a choice. We can go someplace else."

"What's wrong with this place?"

"Look at the name."

"So?"

"This is an insult to Native Americans," she said.

"I really think you're being too sensitive. I'm sure they don't mean anything by it."

"Fine—then let 'em call it Big Cheesy White Guy Auto Sales," she snapped.

"Let's just look around. They might have some good deals."

"Nathan, I'm serious. If you try to force this on me, I'm out of here, and you're on your own."

"I don't see why."

"That's because you're white. You've never had to live with it, but I have, all my life. And I've got to tell you, I'm sick of the Washington Redskins. I'm sick of the Kansas City Chiefs. I'm sick of the Atlanta Braves and their tomahawk chops. These are negative stereotypes that demean my heritage. I'm leaving now—either with you or by myself. What'll it be?"

He had no other choice. "Okay, you win. We'll go someplace else."

A bulky guy wearing a bedraggled feather warbonnet and purple shirt and green pants came smiling out to see them. "Hiya, folks, how's it going?" He put forth a meaty hand. "Joey PaChuko here—I was Big Chief of the Month for May. That means I sold more cars than any other salesman. So you folks are in good hands."

"Get away from me," Jessica warned.

"Gosh, don't have a hissy-fit, sister," Joey said. "Whataya say we smokum the peace pipe?" He winked conspiratorially.

Jessica was so mad she kicked the tires of the nearest car.

"Don't mind her," Nathan said. "She's a little upset about the name of this place. Is there anything nearby where they sell used cars?" Nathan asked.

"There's a car lot about five blocks away from here. It's that way. You can't miss it."

Just to be on the safe side, Nathan asked, "What's it called?"

"Liberty Motors."

Jessica nodded to Nathan to signal her approval. They left Big Chief Auto Sales and started walking.

"You okay?" Nathan asked.

"I'm just really tired of living in a racist society."

"I'm not sure that just calling a place Big Chief Auto Sales is racism."

"What do you call it?"

"Bad taste maybe, but not racism."

"And you, being white, are the final word on what's racist, is that it?" she asked.

"Not really, but I'm pretty sure the owner didn't mean anything by it."

"That makes it even worse."

"What about you? Don't you ever say bad things about whites?"

She glanced at him. "Yeah, I do, actually."

"So maybe you're racist too."

She shook her head. "No. Racism is prejudice plus power. I might be just as prejudiced against whites as some whites are against Indians, but the difference is I don't have any power. So I can't be racist."

"Convenient definition."

"It's the truth. You just can't see it."

Once they made it to Liberty Motors, they walked around the lot for several minutes, waiting for a salesman to come out, but nobody did.

"I know why this is happening," she said.

"Why?"

"It's because of me," she said.

"What are you talking about?"

"It's because I'm Indian."

"I'm sure that doesn't have anything to do with it. Somebody will be out here any minute."

A few more minutes passed by. "Let's go someplace else," she said.

"We can't keep going to one place after another just because you keep imagining people are discriminating against you."

"I'm not imagining this. The fact is that if you were here alone, somebody would have come out by now."

"Everyone is probably busy right now."

A car pulled up. A man got out to look at one of the cars on the lot. A salesman hurried out to talk to him.

"You see what I mean?" she said.

He looked down the street. He could see the sign for another car dealer a block away. "Let's go somewhere else," he said.

Half a block away, she said, "Thanks."

"Sure, no problem."

When they walked onto the lot of the car dealer down the street, she told him to go inside right away while she walked around and looked at the cars.

As he entered, a gray-haired, fatherly type salesman came over.

"We're looking for a car," Nathan said.

"We?"

Nathan glanced out to where Jessica was looking at cars. "My friend and I."

The man looked out and saw Jessica and then asked, "What price range are you thinking of?"

"A used car . . . something around five thousand dollars."

"How about a new car? We can put you on an easy-payment plan."

"No, I'd rather pay cash."

The man's eyebrows raised slightly. "Oh, really?"

"Yes. Is there something wrong with that?"

"No, not at all. What kind of vehicle are you thinking about?"

Nathan thought about giving the car to Jessica after all this was over. "Something she'd like."

"I've got an '86 GMC Jimmy. I could let you have it for fifty-nine hundred dollars."

"Can we take a look at it?"

"Sure thing. Take it for a test drive."

Nathan and Jessica drove it around for a few minutes. Jessica liked it because it would be good on the reservation, even during bad weather because it had four-wheel drive.

"We'll take it," Nathan told the salesman when they returned.

"Great. If you'll come in my office, we can take care of this and get you on your way."

Nathan and the salesman went into a small office while Jessica walked across the street to a convenience store to get some food for their trip.

"I'm going to pay cash," Nathan said.

"All right, fine. Could I just have you fill this out?"

"What is it?"

"We need to transfer title."

"Will you need to see any I.D.?" Nathan asked. He realized he was starting to blush. "The reason I ask is because I lost my wallet just this morning." He had never had much practice lying. He could feel his face turning red.

The salesman handed him a form. "Not really. If you will just fill this out, I'll take care of the rest."

Nathan gave a fictitious name and address.

The salesman looked at Nathan as if he wanted to say something, but then went back to his paperwork. Finally his curiosity got the best of him. "Look, this is none of my business, but you and your . . . friend . . . you look like you're on the run. Is the problem that your parents don't approve of her?"

It was the easiest explanation. "I guess you could say that."

"I think it'd be a lot better to sit down and talk with your folks instead of just running away."

"I've tried to talk with them," Nathan said. "But they just won't listen."

"How long do you think she'll stay with you? Until the money runs out? And then what?"

"Are you saying that just because she's Indian? Because if you are, then that's not right, because you don't know anything about her."

"Just forget I said anything, okay?" The salesman returned to adding up figures on his calculator and came up with a total. Nathan opened up his backpack and laid a stack of hundred-dollar bills on the desk.

"Where'd this come from?" the salesman asked.

"It's what I saved up for college."

"Look, son . . . "

"Do you want my business or not?" Nathan asked.

"I want your business."

"Fine, you've got the money, so are we done?"

"We're done."

"If anyone comes looking for me . . . "

"I'll keep quiet."

"Thanks."

Half an hour later Nathan had a bill of sale and temporary plates, and they were on Interstate 90, heading east.

# CHAPTER FOUR

*Salt Lake City: June 9, 2:30 P.M.*

NATHAN'S FAMILY WAS EXCITEDLY WAITING for Flight 832 from Seattle to land. His parents, Boyd and Elaine; his older brothers, John and Andrew, and their wives and children; his sister, Kim; as well as his grandparents on both sides, and four of his uncles and their wives and children were all milling around on the concourse. Andrew had rented a video camera to record his brother's homecoming.

Under Elaine's direction, the cousins were practicing holding a hand-lettered banner that read "WELCOME HOME, NATHAN!" Kim was holding five helium-filled balloons to give to Nathan when he came through the Jetway.

When Boyd and Elaine first arrived at the airport, they watched a preview of what awaited them. A family, perhaps thirty in all, stood in a group as their son arrived home from his mission and came through a nearby Jetway. Like the Williamses, they also had banners and balloons and a video camera. Elaine's eyes filled with tears as she watched a tall, handsome young man with a big smile run out of the Jetway and into the terminal. He went to his mother first and hugged her and then to his father and then to anyone who happened to be next in the crowd of excited well-wishers.

A young woman stood a short distance apart from the family. Elaine guessed she was the girl who had waited. She seemed unsure of her place in that gathering. Everyone else in the crowd seemed to be family except her.

After hugging everyone, including the babies who had been born since he left on his mission, the missionary saw the young woman standing there, apart from everyone else. He came to her and smiled and shook her hand.

"Aw c'mon," an uncle teased, clapping him on the shoulder. "You can do better than that."

The elder shook his head and said something. Elaine couldn't hear what he said, but she knew what it was. It was the same thing Nathan would say: "I'm not released from my mission yet."

The family went off together, their missionary son at the center of their love.

Elaine smiled because in just a few minutes she also would hold her son in her arms and tell him how happy she was that he was home.

The plane was scheduled to land at 3:20. Just a few minutes to go. After two years, she could wait that long. She had purposely told everyone to come an hour before the plane landed. If she hadn't, she was almost certain that either John or Andrew would arrive late, full of excuses about how busy they were. She didn't want that to happen. She wanted everyone there when Nathan stepped off the plane, not ten or fifteen minutes later. This was Nathan's time to shine.

Nathan was coming home at last. Her youngest son would be back, and their house would come alive once again. Nathan would bring lots of friends home, as he had during his freshman year at Ricks. They'd all crowd into the TV room downstairs, five or ten at a time, watching videos or playing games or singing lustily at the piano. And Nathan would tell her all about his mission, and she'd find out the things he had avoided telling her— times when he and his companion had not gotten along, or maybe some dangerous experiences. She'd hear about the positive experiences too, like times when his prayers had been answered. And she would find out all the countless little things about where he washed his clothes and what it was like to be fleet coordinator. Seated with Nathan at the kitchen table, she would find out, one detail at a time, all about his mission. She would enjoy having her son home until he eventually got married.

She wasn't sure when to let him know about Camille. Maybe she'd tell him about her on the way home to Rexburg. He had trusted her judgment about the suits he bought for his mission. Maybe he'd trust her judgment about Camille. She'd have to be very careful though.

A week earlier she had had a dream in which Nathan and Camille had brought their baby home for the first time. Elaine dreamed she held the child in her arms. She wasn't sure if the dream was a sign or just the product of her own eagerness.

Nathan was her third son. Twice she had watched a son go through courtship and marriage. She knew the rules. She worried that she might become what she had promised herself never to be—an interfering mother. Right now it was enough that her Nathan was coming home. She looked at the clock. It was 2:35.

Her thoughts were interrupted by the agent announcing that Flight 832 from Seattle had been cancelled due to mechanical problems. Passengers on that flight were being rebooked on the next flight, which was scheduled to arrive at seven o'clock.

Everyone in the family was disappointed. To try to at least cheer the younger ones up, Boyd announced he'd buy them all something to eat. They all started for the Burger King inside the terminal.

Boyd was surprised how discouraged Elaine seemed by the delay. "You okay?" he asked.

"Of all the times for this to happen!" she said.

"We waited two years—we can wait another few hours, can't we?"

Elaine nodded. "I suppose. We should have driven to Seattle to get him like we talked about."

"Flying is a lot faster," Boyd said.

"Not at this rate, it isn't."

He put his arm around her shoulder. "Everything's going to be all right, you'll see."

"Yes, of course. Boyd, what do you think about Camille Stoddard?"

"Who's she?"

"She's the girl who comes to clean every Saturday, don't you remember? She attends Ricks."

"Have I ever met her?" Boyd asked.

"I'm sure you have. She's a brunette with short hair, real cute. She looks like that girl on *Northern Exposure.* Sometimes when she works around the house, she sings. She has a wonderful voice."

After twenty-five years of being dragged to vocal recitals, Boyd's eyes glazed over whenever his wife talked about singing.

"Oh, you'll like this about her—she was raised on a farm," Elaine said.

"Is she turning out okay as far as what you need her to do around the place?" Boyd asked.

"Yes, of course."

"What's the problem then?" he asked.

"There's no problem."

"If there's no problem, why are we talking about her?"

"Well, I was just wondering how she and Nathan might get along."

"Nathan's a big boy now. He doesn't need you to help him meet girls."

"I know that—but I really think they'd be perfect together."

He raised his eyebrows. "Our boys have never paid the slightest bit of attention to any suggestion we ever gave 'em about girls. What makes you think that's going to change with Nathan?"

She sighed. "I suppose you're right."

"Of course I'm right."

They stayed at Burger King for as long as they could because there was a TV there for the children. Then one of John's children started feeling sick, so they left. Andrew didn't leave, but he made it clear that he was very busy and had a hundred things to do.

By the time the plane landed, the "WELCOME HOME, NATHAN!" banner had been ripped by Andrew's children, fighting over who was going to hold it. The balloons had all got loose and were now floating against the ceiling. Two grumpy children were holding a crumpled banner that read, "WELCO." Kim was told to hold what was left of the other part; it read "NAT."

Even with all that, they were ready to welcome Nathan home from his mission. The family watched expectantly as each person entered the terminal. But Nathan didn't come. Within two minutes the initial flood of passengers was gone. From then on, passengers entered the concourse one at a time. "So, where is he?" Kim asked her father.

"After two years he probably has a lot of things," he replied. "He'll probably be the very last one."

They waited until no more passengers came out.

Boyd approached the agent at the gate. "We were expecting our son on this flight," he said. "Can you check if anyone is still on the plane?"

She went inside and came out a minute later. "There's nobody else in there."

"I need to know what happened to him."

"It was a nonstop flight, so he must not have gotten on the plane in Seattle."

Boyd returned to his family. "Nathan missed his flight. Maybe he caught a later one."

A sudden wave of panic washed over Elaine. Something was wrong. She knew it.

"If you need to stay overnight, you can stay with us," said Boyd's brother, who lived in nearby Sandy.

"Thanks. We might take you up on that. But first I need to call his mission president and find out if he knows anything."

On the phone Nathan's mission president told Boyd he had seen Nathan get on the plane at about 12:15.

"But that flight was cancelled, so they must have had everyone get off the plane and wait for the later flight," Boyd said. "Nathan must not have gotten on the second plane. That must mean he's still in Seattle. I take it he didn't call you, is that right?"

"No, he didn't."

"Do you know any reason why he'd stay in Seattle?"

"None at all. He was very much looking forward to seeing his family again. He was an exceptional missionary, one of the best

I've ever worked with. I'd never expect him to do anything wrong."

Boyd felt his throat tighten up. Nathan was his "Joseph," his youngest boy, the one most like him of any of his children. He tried not to panic. "Could you check with the other missionaries to make sure he's not staying with them for the night?"

"Yes, I'll do that right away."

"Thank you. I'll call back later tonight," Boyd said.

Returning to where the family was waiting, Boyd tried to report what he had learned without appearing to be alarmed.

"What did you find out?" Elaine asked anxiously.

"His mission president saw him get on the earlier plane. But then they must have taken everybody off to wait for the later flight. Nathan obviously missed that."

"Why would he stay in Seattle when he knows we're here waiting for him?"

"I don't know. Maybe he just missed it. He could have fallen asleep or something like that."

"When's the next plane?" Elaine asked.

"I asked. The next Delta flight from Seattle isn't until tomorrow morning."

"Where is he going to sleep tonight?" Elaine asked.

"I'm sure he'll call the mission office and make arrangements."

"Has he done that?"

"Not yet. But he might have made arrangements with his old companion or some of the other elders he's worked with. His mission president is going to check with all the elders in the area."

"Something's happened to him, hasn't it," Kim said.

Boyd looked at Kim. From the time she was little, she seemed to have a sixth sense. Sometimes she scared him by the things she seemed to know before anyone else. He didn't even want to know what she might be feeling now, in case it was very bad.

"I don't know."

They checked all the other airlines for the times of their flights from Seattle. There were other ways to get to Salt Lake

City from Seattle, but none was direct, as was the one Nathan should have been on.

Andrew eventually took his family and left to go home. His children had gotten restless and unruly. But just to be on the safe side, Boyd, Elaine, and Kim waited in the terminal until 10:30, then called the mission president again. This time Boyd let Elaine talk to him because she was better at asking all the questions that needed to be asked. The mission president said that neither he nor any of the missionaries had heard from Nathan. His last companion had even checked with several members of the ward they attended; nobody had seen or heard from Nathan.

"Is there any chance he might have gone to visit someone he met on his mission?" Elaine asked.

"For two years I've always been able to depend on your son to do the right thing. I can't imagine him breaking mission rules on the last day of his mission."

"Have you checked your local hospitals?" she asked.

"Yes, we have. Nobody matches Nathan's description."

"Have you contacted the police?"

"Yes, just a few minutes ago. We've alerted them to Nathan's possible disappearance, but they have no report or any news of him at this time."

"If he calls, please let him stay with you and we'll drive up and get him."

"Of course. Can you give me a number where you can be reached tonight?"

She gave him the phone number of Boyd's brother in Sandy.

"I think it would be well to notify the Church Missionary Department and get them involved," the mission president said. "I'll give them a call as soon as we hang up."

"Yes. Please do," she said weakly. "Thank you for all your help. We'll call you in the morning. Good-bye." She hung up and stared out the window into the darkness of the night. "Our son is missing," she said.

# CHAPTER FIVE

*Interstate 90: June 9*

NATHAN AND JESSICA TRAVELED EAST ON INTERSTATE 90. About an hour from Seattle, he saw an auto salvage yard from the interstate. He took the next exit and drove back to it. While Jessica distracted the owner's son in the office, he drove around the rows of junked cars until he found a wrecked Ford Bronco with current license plates. Feeling guilty, Nathan removed the plates and put them under the seat of the Jimmy. It felt like he was stealing, but he remembered what Gibbs had told him about how vicious Steiger and Donovan were. *Maybe,* he thought, *this is kind of like Nephi being commanded to slay Laban.* Then he removed a few other parts so he'd have something to buy when he returned to where Jessica was still talking with the owner's son. A few minutes later they were on their way again, but only to the next rest area, where they pulled in and put the stolen plates on the Jimmy. Now Steiger would have a hard time finding them by tracing their license plates.

Nathan insisted on driving. Jessica didn't mind; she hadn't slept much the night before anyway, so she climbed into the backseat and went to sleep.

At ten o'clock that night, they entered Idaho. He realized he was right on schedule—it was just two years since he'd left on his mission. But this was not the way he thought he would be returning to his home state.

If things were different, he could be home for breakfast. He'd introduce Jessica—his family would like her—and then in the morning he'd go visit with his stake president and explain what had happened. Maybe later in the day he'd go out with his dad to look around the farm. But sometime, maybe later that night or the next day or a week later, the full realization would come to him of the danger he had put his family in. From then on he'd always be looking over his shoulder for Steiger to show up and wipe out everything he held dear.

*I can't go home,* he thought.

Around two o'clock in the morning, he stopped for gas. He was too tired to drive, so he traded places with Jessica. She took over the wheel while he curled up in back to sleep.

Suddenly he woke up and looked at his watch. It was three-thirty in the morning. The Jimmy was parked outside a motel office, and Jessica was inside at the counter filling out a card. A few minutes later she came out and got back in the driver's seat.

"Where are we?" he asked.

"Bozeman."

"Why did you stop here?" Nathan asked.

"We're both too tired to drive, so I got us a place to sleep for a while."

Nathan found it hard to talk or think that late at night. "Both of us in the same room?" he asked, his voice cracking.

"Don't worry—there're two beds."

"Can't we get two rooms?"

"This is the last room they had. We're lucky to get it. It's the bridal suite, but they let me have it for the regular price."

Even as exhausted as he was, something didn't make sense. "They have a bridal suite with two beds?"

"The couch makes up into a bed. It'll be okay. Besides, if we keep driving, we're going to have an accident. We'll sleep with what we have on now. It won't be any different than what we've been doing except that we'll both be asleep at the same time. You'll be in one bed, and I'll be in the other. It'll be okay."

"Why didn't you just pull off at a rest stop?"

"I had an aunt who got robbed in the middle of the night at a rest stop. It's not like we don't have the money to pay for it. Just take a look at the room. It's probably huge. We won't even see each other all night. It'll work out. You'll see."

She drove over to their room and parked. As she unlocked the door to the room, a dozen alarms went off in his head. She opened the door and stepped in. "You coming in?"

He hesitated. "I shouldn't be here with you."

"Oh, come on, Nathan. Do you really think I'm going to put a move on you while you're sleeping?"

"No."

"Well, if it's not that, what is it? Look, just come in and see. The room's big. We'll each have our own part all to ourselves."

He walked in. She was right—it was a big room. "You want to use the bathroom?" she asked.

"I guess so."

A few minutes later, as he washed up, he looked around the bathroom. Behind him was a sunken hot tub. The bath mat was in the shape of a heart. He opened a free sample of toothpaste and brushed his teeth with his finger. He'd left everything—his suitcase, his clothes, his razor, his scriptures, everything—back in Seattle.

He looked at himself in the mirror and wondered how he'd ever gotten into this. In one day he had become an accomplice in knocking an FBI agent unconscious, walked out of a plane carrying the FBI agent's gun, been given ten thousand dollars to hold a computer disk for a man he didn't know, and now he was in a motel room about to spend the night with a girl he hardly knew.

Suspicions about Jessica once again crept into his mind. Why was it so important to her that they stay the night here? Was she planning on killing him in his sleep? Or was this just a delaying tactic? Once he fell asleep, would she sneak out and contact Steiger by phone? Would Steiger then come and kill him in his sleep?

Strangely enough, it was easier for him to believe she would kill him during the night than that she would try to seduce him.

Even if she weren't working for Steiger, and even if nothing wrong was going to take place while they were spending the night in the same motel room, he knew it was not right for him to be there with her. He knew what his parents' reaction would be, and his mission president's. He knew what he needed to do.

When he came out of the bathroom, she asked, "You want the bed or the couch?"

He shook his head. "This isn't right."

"What do you mean?"

"I'm still a missionary. I'm not even supposed to be alone with you."

"Nathan, c'mon. You've been alone with me since we left Seattle."

"I know, but this is different."

"How is it different?"

"What will people think if they find out we spent the night together in a honeymoon suite?"

"What? You think I planned all along that we'd end up here tonight? I told you before—this was the last room they had."

"What would my mom and dad say if they knew this is where I was?"

"Do you think your mom and dad would want us falling asleep at the wheel and having an accident?"

"No, but they also wouldn't want me to sleep in the same motel room with you."

"I trust *you.* Why don't you trust *me?*" she asked.

"I trust you."

"Then what's the problem? We can get a good night's sleep on a bed, or we can hurt our necks and backs sleeping in the Jimmy. Since we've already paid for the room, I think this is the best thing for us to do. Let me get ready for bed in the bathroom while you think about what you want to do. We can talk about it when I come out."

Nathan was frustrated because for every reason he gave her why he couldn't stay, she came up with a reason why it would be okay. But then he realized he didn't have to win a debate to do what he knew was best. All he had to do was to act on his convictions. "Wait," he said.

She stopped.

"I have no business being here with you. That's the way I feel, and nothing you say is going to change that. So you stay here, and I'll grab a blanket and a pillow and go out and sleep in the Jimmy."

"You sure?"

"I'm sure."

"Okay, Nathan, if that's the way you feel."

He grabbed a blanket from the closet and a pillow from the large circular bed and left. Rolling up in the blanket in the cramped backseat of the Jimmy, he knew he had done the right thing.

▼ ▼ ▼

*Bozeman, Montana: Friday, June 10*

Nathan was awakened the next morning by a family getting into a car parked next to the Jimmy.

"Daddy, there's a dead person in there," a young girl said.

"He's not dead," her father said, looking in at Nathan. "He's just sleeping."

"He must have been real bad for his daddy to make him stay out here," the little girl continued.

"I think you're right, Sarah. He must have been real bad."

"What do you think he did, Daddy?"

"I don't know. What do you think he did?"

"I think he blew bubbles in his milk with his straw and made a big mess. That's what I think he did."

"You're probably right."

Jessica came outside to talk to him at ten that morning. "Nathan, I'm done in there. Do you want to take a shower and get cleaned up? I'll wait out here for you."

"Okay, thanks."

"Give me the keys and some money and I'll go get gas and clean the windshield."

He saw her off and then went to talk to the desk clerk of the motel. "I forgot my razor," he said. "Do you have one I can use?"

"What room are you in?"

Nathan showed him the room key. The man at the desk

smiled. "Oh yes, the bridal suite. Your lovely bride borrowed a toothbrush just a few minutes ago. You're a lucky man. Yes sir, no question about that."

Nathan felt himself turning red. "Can I get a toothbrush too?"

"Both of you forgot to pack your toothbrushes, hey? Must have had your mind on something else. Hey? Right? Huh? Am I right?"

Nathan grabbed the razor and toothbrush and escaped.

After he showered, he had to put on the same clothes he'd worn the day before. That made him miss his suitcase again.

Jessica was waiting in the Jimmy when he left the room. They pulled out of the motel parking lot and stopped at McDonald's for breakfast, and then got back on the interstate. He drove; she sat in front with him.

"Well, we got through that okay, didn't we?" she said, referring to the previous night.

"Yeah, we did."

"I've never met a guy like you before. Why are you so different?"

He shrugged his shoulders. "I guess it's the way I was brought up. My dad's taught me a lot of things."

"Like what?"

"Like how to work and how to live. And if you make a promise to someone, then you need to keep it. I've made a promise to God about chastity."

"Is that part of your religion?"

"Yeah, it is."

"That's good. I made a promise like that too, once. Someday, maybe I'll tell you about it."

"I bet your folks are proud of the way you've turned out," he said.

For a long time she didn't say anything and then, almost too quietly to be heard, she said, "My dad ran out on my mom and me when I was ten. Things really went downhill for us after that. I wish I could have had a dad like yours. You don't want to ever disappoint him, do you."

"No," he agreed.

"That's really good. You know what? I think we might end up being good friends."

They looked at each other and smiled. "I think so, too," he said.

They stopped for lunch in Billings at one-thirty. When they were ready to take off again, Jessica asked if he wanted her to drive, but he said he was okay. She decided to get in the backseat and sleep so she'd be wide-awake when he needed a break.

On a long stretch of interstate, he adjusted his mirror so he could watch her as she slept. She was lying on her side facing toward him. She had used her leather jacket as a pillow and her head rested on one arm. As she slept her lips were slightly parted.

*She's an Indian,* he thought. *I'm going to stay on the reservation with an Indian. When my ancestors crossed the plains to go to Utah, they might have passed her ancestors. What if I'd been alive then? What if I'd seen her then? What if I'd been out riding ahead of the wagon train and had come across her? What would I have done? Dismissed her as some ignorant savage, the way some people did in those days? I hope not. I hope I'd have stopped to talk to her. But how would we have ever communicated?*

*There is so much grace and beauty in her face,* he thought. *She walks with a simple elegance, keeping her shoulders back and head erect. Is that because she's Indian or because she's Miss Indian America?*

She woke up a few minutes later and sat up and asked him to stop soon because she needed to use a rest room. He saw a rest stop just ahead. He pulled off the highway and stopped, and they both went in to use their separate rest rooms. By the time he returned to the Jimmy, she was sitting in the driver's seat. He got in on the passenger side.

"What were you looking at with the mirror like this?" she teased.

He turned bright red.

"Elder Williams, were you looking at me while I was sleeping?"

"I was just making sure . . . that . . . " He struggled for an excuse. "That . . . "

He gave up. She'd caught him, and there was no getting out of it. "Yes."

"Why?"

He was embarrassed but finally stammered, "I really like . . . the way you look."

She shrugged her shoulders. "I don't mind. Really, it's okay. You can look at me all you want." Then she became embarrassed as she realized that what she had said could be taken the wrong way. "What I mean is . . . I'm not threatened by you like I am some guys." She was embarrassed enough to want to change the subject. "How about if I drive? You get in the back and sleep. I'll wake you up when I get tired."

He tried to sleep, but it was no good. He kept worrying about his parents. He had to let them know he was all right. But how? Gibbs had told him not to phone or write home because any message he sent would be intercepted. Steiger might be able to trace calls going into his parents' place and even read every piece of mail before it was delivered, but Nathan didn't see how he could monitor every phone call going into Idaho. *All I have to do,* he thought, *is phone somebody and ask them to let my parents know I'm okay.*

He tried to think of the least likely person who could get a message to his folks. He thought about the girl who delivered their newspaper. She had been doing it for the past three years. She was fourteen when he left on his mission. He never would have paid much attention to her, but one Sunday morning when he went to get the paper wearing only pajama bottoms, he had opened the door and there she was staring at him. They had both been embarrassed and never mentioned it to anyone else. But after that, Nathan began to notice her.

What was her name? Her family lived just down the block. They were in the same ward. Finally he remembered her last name was Myers. But what was her first name? He tried to remember but couldn't. It probably didn't matter. He could find it out when he called. That's what he'd do the next time they stopped. He'd phone her and give her a message for his parents.

With that settled, he was finally able to fall asleep.

He woke up just outside Sheridan, Wyoming. They switched places again.

At seven that night they reached Spearfish, South Dakota. They were both hungry, so they stopped at McDonald's. He told Jessica about his plan to call the Myers girl. After they finished eating, he went outside to use a pay phone. He got Myers's phone number from directory assistance. Jessica put her arm around his waist and her ear next to the phone so she could hear. Nathan wished she wasn't so close, but he knew she didn't mean anything by it. It was just her way.

The girl's father in Rexburg answered the phone. "Hello."

Nathan's voice cracked from nervousness. "I need to talk to your daughter. My paper wasn't delivered today."

"Trish hasn't delivered papers for two years."

Nathan didn't know what to say. His voice cracked again. "I still need to talk to her."

"Why? What business do you have with my daughter?" Mr. Myers asked. He sounded angry.

"I . . . uh . . . "

"Who are you, anyway?"

"I can't tell you who I am," Nathan said.

"Then you can't talk to my daughter. I don't know what you're up to, but don't call back or I'll have you thrown in jail for harassment." And with that he hung up.

"Struck out, huh?" Jessica asked.

"Yeah, pretty much."

A car pulled up, and two young men in suits got out and walked toward the restaurant entrance. Nathan saw their missionary name tags and immediately felt guilty. Jessica was leaning against him with her hand on his forearm. He pulled away from her. As the missionaries passed by, one of them caught Nathan's eye and said hello. Then they went inside. Nathan's face was wet with perspiration.

Jessica moved away from him. "You still feel guilty being with me, don't you." It was a statement, not a question.

"Yes."

"Why?"

"It's against mission rules."

"Nathan, you're not a missionary anymore."

"I'm a missionary until I report to my stake president."

"And if you could, you would have done it yesterday, right?"

"Yes."

"And if you'd done it yesterday, then today it would be all right for us to eat together at McDonald's?"

"Yes."

"If you're feeling so bad about this, why don't you call this stake president you keep talking about and ask him to tell you it's all right now for you to be like everybody else."

"Gibbs said not to call anyone."

"You just called someone," she pointed out.

"Yes, but they might *expect* me to call my stake president. They wouldn't expect me to call the girl who delivered our newspaper two years ago."

"Okay, we're back to the girl again. Do you want me to try calling her?"

"Yeah, please." He handed her the phone receiver and the paper on which he'd written the phone number and told her the name to use. Jessica punched out the numbers. "Hello, can I talk to Trish?" she said when Mr. Myers answered. He called Trish, and a moment later she came on the phone.

"Trish," Jessica said, "I have a big surprise for you. Hold on, okay?" She gave the phone to Nathan.

"Trish, this is Nathan Williams. Remember me? Kim is my sister. Look, I need you to tell my folks I'm okay. I can't come home for a few weeks, but I'm okay. Tell 'em not to worry. But look, you can't phone 'em because people are listening into all their phone calls. And you can't write 'em a letter either because they're reading all their mail. You'll have to catch 'em where there's no chance anyone can be listening in, okay? And it has to be today or tomorrow at the latest. Can you do that for me?"

Nathan had been talking too fast, and he wondered if he had made any sense.

"Okay, sure," Trish said.

"That'd be great. Oh, also, would you please tell President Anderson that I'd like him to release me from my mission, but that I can't meet with him for a while. I'll tell him all about it when I see him. Will you tell him that?"

"Okay."

"And Trish, you can't tell anyone else about this, not even your parents."

"Okay."

"Great. Thanks a lot. Be sure and let my parents know I'm okay."

They both said good-bye and hung up.

"How old is Trish?" Jessica asked.

"Sixteen."

"I think you two have a great future together."

"Very funny."

"I'm serious. She's Mormon, isn't she?"

"Yeah, why?"

"That's half the battle with you people, isn't it?" she teased.

"I don't make fun of your beliefs, do I?"

"I wasn't making fun of your beliefs. You will marry a Mormon though, won't you?"

"Yes."

"That's what I thought. I guess in a way I'm like you. The man I marry will be a full-blood. I want to preserve the blood-line."

Through the window Nathan watched the elders. He thought how simple it would be if he were still on his mission—to be on his way back to the apartment after a day spent talking with people about the Church, discussing with his companion the people they had talked to, and then having evening prayer with his companion, sleeping soundly, waking up, studying the scriptures, having a study class together, and then getting back out on the street, going tracting and working to set up more discussions.

"You wish you could tag along with them, don't you?" Jessica asked.

"Yeah, I do," he said. He couldn't seem to take his eyes off the two missionaries. It was as though he had died or was invisible and was gazing at what his life had been in better days.

"What was so great about being a missionary?" she asked.

"Knowing we were God's messengers. It was wonderful, Jessica. When we did our best, he'd honor the promises we made to people."

"What kind of promises?"

"That they'd recover from being sick, that God would help them quit smoking, that if they paid tithing, God would bless them and they'd end up with so many blessings that they wouldn't have room for them all."

Her eyebrows raised. "You promised people things like *that?*"

"Yes."

"Promise *me* something," she said.

He cleared his throat. "What?"

"I'm serious. I'm risking my life for you. That ought to be worth something. So give me a promise like that."

Nathan searched within himself for the gift he had had on his mission, to give priesthood blessings, to make promises that if the people accepted the challenges he gave them, they would be blessed. When he had given such promises, he knew within himself they would be honored.

But the feeling was gone, the assurance was gone, the confidence was gone, and the calling as a missionary was gone. Nathan knew that the same way he knew so many things that came with the Church, by the Spirit. Suddenly it seemed clear to him. His mission was over and he didn't need to live the mission rules any longer. He was relieved to feel that what he was doing was not wrong.

"I can't give you any promises," he said.

"Why not?"

"Because I'm not a missionary anymore."

"That's what I've been trying to tell you," she said.

"I know. You were right."

The elders finished eating and got up to leave. Nathan realized this might be his last chance to get a copy of the Book of Mormon. He'd left his scriptures on the plane in Seattle.

As the two came out to their car, Nathan went up to them. "I was wondering if you have a copy of the Book of Mormon. She's not a member," he said, pointing to Jessica.

Both elders broke into a big smile. They went to the trunk of their car and got Jessica a copy. Nathan offered to pay them, but they refused.

"Where are you two from?" one of the missionaries asked.

"Oh, you know, just around." Because he didn't want them thinking he and Jessica were living together, he said, "Jessica here is my cousin."

The missionary looked at Nathan and then at Jessica and then asked, "So . . . you're both Indian, is that right?"

"That's right," Nathan said.

Jessica started giggling. Nathan didn't want to explain anything else, so he said good-bye and got in the Jimmy and started it up.

Jessica was still laughing as they drove out of the parking lot.

▼ ▼ ▼

They made it to Rapid City by eight that night. They needed to buy camping gear, food, and, because they'd both lost their luggage, more clothing.

Jessica drove them to a large mall near the interstate. They found nearly everything they needed there. They bought clothes, camping equipment, and a few other items, then loaded everything into the Jimmy. Before they left, Nathan told Jessica he needed to go back. When she asked why, he said he needed to look around some more. He gave her some money to shop for whatever she needed; then he went to the sporting goods section.

A clerk approached him. "May I help you?"

Nathan pulled Steiger's gun from his daypack. "I need some bullets for this gun."

"What size?"

"Good question. A friend gave this to me but didn't tell me anything about it, and I don't know anything about guns."

"Let me take a look." The salesclerk picked up the gun. "That's a snub-nosed .38."

"Okay, great, thanks."

"How many rounds do you need?"

"I don't know. How many are in a box?"

"Fifty."

"Five boxes ought to be enough."

"Going to do a lot of shooting?"

"I hope not."

After buying ammunition, he drifted over to the hardware section. He saw a boy there with his father; they were buying tools. Nathan picked up a three-eighths-inch wrench. His father was so big that a wrench like that almost became lost in his hands. He realized then how much he wanted to be with his dad again out on the farm, working side by side. He wanted to be home. It had been too long. He had forgotten what it was like to walk into the house and smell bread baking, or to have his mom drive out to the fields at noon to bring cold meat-loaf sandwiches made of bread just out of the oven, along with a large thermos of lemonade made from real lemons. And her smile. He loved his mother's smile; it was there for him whenever he walked into the house.

Jessica found him standing in the hardware section with the wrench in his hand. She waited patiently until he gently, almost reverently, set the wrench back down. Then they left the store.

On their way out of town, Jessica had Nathan stop at the South Dakota School of Mines and Technology to show him around. Although the library was closed, she had keys that would get them into the Native American Study Center on the unfinished third floor of the library. To him it wasn't that great—a small room partitioned off in the middle of a large empty room whose walls and floors were concrete. Inside the modular, partitioned room were two long study tables and a computer. A decorated elk hide and a star quilt had been hung on the walls.

"What do you think?" she asked.

"I see a few chairs and a couple of tables and a computer. It's not half as nice as what I saw on the first floor. But when you talk about it, your eyes light up. So I must be missing something here. Why is this so important to you?"

"Because this is home for us. This is where we can kick back and be ourselves."

"Why can't you be yourself on the first floor?" he asked.

"I'll try to explain it to you, but you have to try to understand something," she said.

"What?"

"You don't know what it's like for us."

"I can guess what it's like."

"No, that's just it, you can't," she said.

"Why not?"

"Because you're white. The sooner you accept the fact that you can't know what it's like for an American Indian, or an African-American, or a Hispanic, the quicker you'll come to understand why we say the things we say."

He didn't agree with her, but he could see she wasn't going to give in, so he decided to go along with her and see where it led. "Okay, I'll accept that for now."

"I'm serious. You take a Lakota student coming here as a freshman. He's grown up on the reservation, and goes to class for the first time. He sees white students all around him. The instructor is white. He's the only 'Skin."

"'Skin?"

"I can say that, but don't you ever say it. To you we're American Indian or Native American. Anyway, class ends and all the white students go off together in groups to do the homework. They don't talk to the Indian freshman. They don't ask him to study with them. He's totally isolated. That kid, no matter how smart he is, will be lucky if he lasts the semester. And when he's in trouble, where does he go? Who does he talk to? He's not going to go to the dean of students for counseling, and he's not going to go to the instructor and ask for help with his homework. He's just going to pack up and go back to the reservation. And it's not that he can't do the work. He can. He's smart enough. But the thing that's happened to him is what we call ethnic isolation. The

School of Mines used to lose five or so of its Indian students in the first week of class every year. One time one of our freshmen was standing outside the library, and a man who worked on campus came up and asked if she was lost. What kind of a message do you think she got from that? You think that made her feel welcome? Things like that go on all the time in this town."

Nathan had been with Jessica for two days, and only now did he feel like he was really seeing her. It was almost as if she had taken off a mask she had been wearing the whole time she was on the plane and during the drive east. But now, in this place, she seemed more alive. "So I take it that because of the study center, you don't lose as many," he said.

"That's right, as long as we can get them to come here. We have some of our juniors and seniors work with the freshmen on their algebra or trigonometry or calculus or chemistry. When they're here, they're part of a community. If this study center wasn't here, then they'd feel isolated, and eventually a lot of them would be washed out. And then some of the white professors would think, 'I knew they didn't belong here. They're better off doing beadwork or making baskets. That's where their real talents are.'"

"It looks to me like you're giving these students special treatment. What do you say to the people who say they think you should give equal treatment to everybody and not do something for one group of people that you're not willing to do for all people?"

She pretended to be choking him.

"I take it that's a question you've been asked before," he said.

"All the time. And on the surface it sounds good to say you're going to treat everybody equally."

"But?"

"You put one isolated Indian student in a class of forty whites with a white professor, and he or she is not going to feel like they've got an equal chance. But if you put three together in the same class and you get them to work together and help each other out, then they feel more like they can survive. You can say what you want, but the way we're doing it works."

He still wasn't convinced. "But aren't you going the wrong way with these students? Shouldn't you be trying to integrate them instead of segregating them?"

"We lose most of our students during their freshman year. So we have to help them get through that. Usually, by the time they're juniors and seniors they fit in with any group on campus."

"You love it here, don't you," he said.

"Yes, I really do. I spend as much time here as I can. Our freshmen are the hope of the future, and I love working with them."

"You are a warrior for your people, like you said."

She nodded. "I am a woman of destiny for my people."

He looked into her eyes and could see the depth of her commitment. She was as dedicated to what she felt was her mission in life as he was to his. "In some ways we're a lot the same," he said.

"I've noticed that."

It was eleven that night when they finally left for the reservation. Because she was familiar with the roads, she drove. After leaving Rapid City, they saw few cars on the road. It took them an hour and a half to get to Kyle. She pulled into the parking lot of a school.

"This is Little Wound School," she said. "I graduated from here. I'm working days here this summer as a custodian. Oh, the outside of the building is shaped like a buffalo. I'll take you in sometime and show you around. I've got keys, so we can get in anytime we want."

"I don't see a buffalo."

"We'll come back sometime, okay?" She pulled out and they drove slowly through the town. There were only a couple of stores and a gas station, and that was about it.

They continued on the highway for a few more miles, and then she turned onto a gravel road. She followed the road for a short distance, then turned onto a dirt road still furrowed with ruts from spring. By this time they were going only about ten miles an hour. Jessica seemed to know every rut and bump in the road.

She pointed to a small, run-down house off the road. "That's where my grandmother lives. It's not much, but she likes it."

She continued up a hill, following the road up a draw. About two hundred yards from her grandmother's house, she pulled into a hilly, wooded area and stopped. "This is it."

Nathan grabbed the flashlight they had bought in town, and they got out of the Jimmy.

"I stayed near here once," Jessica said.

"What for?"

"I was going through a hard time and needed to get away by myself to think. I fasted for a couple of days."

"What for?"

"I was seeking a vision . . . not far from here . . . higher up, on a cliff of the butte."

"Did you get one?"

"Yes."

"What was in your vision?"

"That's not something I talk about," she said quietly.

"Sure. I understand."

She brightened. "But this is a good place for visions. Maybe you'll have one while you're here."

"Maybe so."

Five minutes later they had unpacked everything. "You need any help putting up the tent?" she asked.

"No, thanks. I'll be fine."

"Okay. I hope you've got everything you need. There are three jerry cans of water. I'll come back tomorrow night and bring some more. Anything else you can think of?"

"No, this'll be great. Thanks a lot."

"You going to be okay here?"

"Sure. Besides, it's just for two weeks."

Nathan didn't even bother to set up the tent. He unrolled his new sleeping bag on the ground and crawled into it. The sky was full of stars, just like back home in Idaho.

# CHAPTER SIX

*Salt Lake City: Friday, June 10, 9:30 P.M.*

BOYD AND ELAINE WILLIAMS WATCHED the last passenger disembark from the last flight that day from Seattle. It was the fourth flight they had met that day. Now they were alone. Everyone else in the family had abandoned them. Even Kim had asked if she could stay with her cousins rather than spend another minute at the airport.

They had done everything they could think of. Early that morning they had talked again to Nathan's mission president. He had heard nothing. The police had nothing to report.

In the afternoon, between flights from Seattle, they had gone to the Church Office Building to talk to the people in the Missionary Department. The man they talked to said the Church would publish Nathan's picture and description in a missing person's bulletin that would go out the next week to all bishops and stake presidents. And then they had gone back to the airport to wait for the next flight from Seattle—and the next. Again, no Nathan.

Elaine's eyes were red and bloodshot, and Boyd had a dull ache in his stomach that signaled his ulcer was acting up again.

"What are we going to do now?" Elaine asked.

"I don't know. We can call the police in Seattle again, I guess. I don't know what else to do."

"I want my boy back," she said. Her voice betrayed how close she was to losing control.

"I know. I do too. Maybe we should go home and see if there's any messages on the machine. Maybe Nathan called us at home and left a message."

"Isn't there some way we can phone home and get our messages?" she asked.

Boyd felt as if his mind were encased in molasses. "I think so, but I've never done it."

When it came to anything electronic, they had always depended on Nathan to figure it out. "If Nathan were here . . . " Elaine never finished the sentence, but burst into tears.

Boyd put his arm around her. "Let's go home, so we'll be there when Nathan calls," he said.

"What if he comes in on the first flight tomorrow morning?"

"He'll call us and we'll go get him. We can't spend the rest of our lives here."

"It won't come to that, will it?"

"No, of course not. Look at it this way. When he does call us, he'll call us at home, so we need to be there. Maybe he's already left a message, and we'll hear it the minute we walk into the house. Or maybe he'll be there waiting for us. Maybe somehow he got a flight directly to Rexburg. I'm sure it's something like that."

"I know my Nathan. He wouldn't put us through this kind of torture unless something had happened to him."

"I'm sure that when we find out what it is, everything will make sense. Someday we'll probably even laugh about this."

"I keep wondering if he's been hurt and is lying along the side of some road. You hear about things like that all the time, but it's always happening to someone else. Maybe this time it's happening to us."

"It's not happening to us," Boyd said impatiently. "Let's just go home."

They picked up Kim and arrived in Rexburg a little after two-thirty A.M. Kim was asleep in the backseat when they pulled into the driveway. Boyd and Elaine ran inside. Their answering machine was blinking. It blinked once for each message. There were three messages.

Elaine punched Play.

First message: "Hello! This is Bishop Murdock. Nathan, welcome home! We've heard so many wonderful things about the great job you did on your mission. I'm looking forward to seeing you again. Oh, one other thing, I just wanted to make sure you know you're scheduled to speak in sacrament meeting this Sunday. You're the main speaker, so you'll have about thirty minutes. We were also wondering if you'd speak to the priests in priesthood meeting. Take as much time as you'd like. Let me know if that's all right."

Second message: "Sister Williams, this is Camille. I must have been confused because I came for my singing lesson today and you weren't there. I knew you and your family had gone to pick up your son in Salt Lake, but I thought you'd be home by now. I guess it must have taken longer than you thought it would. We can reschedule it for next week. Oh, do you want me to come Saturday to help clean?"

Third message: "This is Trish Myers." There was a long pause, and then the voice continued. "Would it be all right if I came and jumped on your trampoline tomorrow? Thanks."

There were no more messages. They both stared at the answering machine. Then Elaine broke down. "He should have called! Why didn't he? I can't stand not knowing! Where is he? Is he even alive? Why haven't we heard something? He should have called. You promised he'd call . . . " She was sobbing uncontrollably. Boyd tried to comfort her, but it was no use.

He went out to the car and woke Kim up and unpacked the car. Then he went back outside and sat on a lawn chair and looked at the stars and wondered if the same stars were looking down on his son somewhere. He stayed there until long after the light in their bedroom had gone out. Then he walked silently back inside and went to bed. He had a hard time falling asleep, but when he did, he kept dreaming the phone was ringing. When he picked it up, no one was ever on the other end.

▼ ▼ ▼

*Rexburg, Idaho: Saturday, June 11*

Boyd postponed doing any work until eleven the next day, but finally he decided to go replace a worn-out sprinkler head he'd noticed earlier in the week. While he was working on it, the cellular phone rang. He picked it up.

"We've got some word on Nathan!" Elaine exclaimed. "He's alive! Come home as soon as you can!"

"I'll be right there." He jumped into his truck and drove the four miles home in record time, leaving a long cloud of dust behind him. When he entered the house, Elaine and Trish Myers were in the kitchen talking.

"Would you mind telling my husband what you told me?" Elaine asked.

Trish was turning into a real beauty. She looked like a tall, modest Daryl Hannah. When she was nervous, she liked to play with her hair. She was nervous now. "There's not much to tell. Last night there were two phone calls for me. The first one my dad picked up. It was a guy. I think it was Nathan. He told my dad that he hadn't received a newspaper and he wanted to talk to me. My dad told him I hadn't delivered the papers for two years, but the guy said he still needed to talk to me. When Dad asked his name, he wouldn't give it, so Dad hung up on him. And then a little while later this girl called. My dad answered it. She asked for me, and when I said hello, she said she had a surprise for me. Then Nathan came on the phone. He told me to tell you guys that he's okay but that he can't come home for a few weeks."

"Did he say why he can't come home?"

"No. But he also asked me to talk to President Anderson and tell him he needed to be released from his mission."

"Why did he call you?" Boyd asked.

"He said he thought people would be listening in to your phone calls."

"What people?"

"He didn't say."

"Did he say where he was going or where he was phoning from?" Elaine asked.

"No, but I could hear cars going by, so I guess it was right by a highway."

"Did he say he'd call back again?" Boyd asked.

"No, he didn't."

"Was there anything unusual about the girl who talked to you first?" Elaine asked.

"Not really."

"Think hard," Boyd said.

"Well, she had kind of a low voice and she talked different."

"In what way?"

"I don't know how to describe it."

"Was it a Southern accent?"

"No."

"Did she sound like she was from the East?" Elaine asked.

"No."

"Have you talked to President Anderson?" Boyd asked.

"No. Do you want me to?"

"No, we'll talk to him."

▼ ▼ ▼

"What do you make of it?" President Anderson asked after hearing about the phone call Trish Myers had received.

"We're not sure. His mission president let me speak with Nathan's last companion," Boyd said. "I asked him if Nathan might have met a girl in Seattle. He told me they hadn't even been teaching any single girls. He said he can't imagine how Nathan might have met anybody without him knowing about it."

"Apparently he's with a girl now, though," President Anderson said.

"Yes, he's with a girl, and they were somewhere near a highway."

"Nathan's a good boy. He hasn't done anything wrong, and he won't do anything wrong," Elaine said.

President Anderson looked at Elaine soberly. Though he didn't say so, he wondered if Nathan might not have gotten himself improperly involved with some young woman.

Reading the president's thoughts, Elaine said firmly, "I know my son."

▼ ▼ ▼

*Seattle: June 11, 9:30 A.M.*

The first thing Steiger did when he got to his office that morning was to look at the printout generated by the CASEE machine. Computer Assisted Sorting and Electronic Ear—an electronic surveillance device—allows law enforcement agencies to monitor all phone calls coming into an entire city.

Steiger was monitoring calls into Rexburg, Idaho, looking for the key words: *Nathan, Williams, Gibbs, FBI,* and *drugs.* At the same time he was also monitoring all phone calls to Nathan's family.

A short time later he entered Donovan's office. "Gibbs's boy phoned home," he said.

"When?"

"Last night."

"Where was he when he called?"

"Spearfish, South Dakota."

"Any idea where he's going?"

Steiger glanced at the list of passengers who had been on Flight 832. "When I got on the plane and found Gibbs, the Williams kid was sitting in the same row with a girl from South Dakota. Maybe she's taking him home."

"Sounds like a good possibility," Donovan said.

"You want me to go take care of that now?"

"Not yet. Your first job is to get rid of Gibbs, and then you can go after Williams and the girl."

Steiger smiled. "I'm not too worried. The way I see it, sooner or later, all roads lead to me."

"That's not a road, then," Donovan joked.

"What is it?"

"A dead end."

# CHAPTER SEVEN

*Pine Ridge Reservation, South Dakota: June 11*

NATHAN WOKE TO THE SOUND OF ROBINS. As he sat up, he saw everything scattered about him on the ground. There was a lot of work that needed to be done to set up his camp the way he'd been taught in Scouting.

Because he was worried about someone flying over the area looking for him, he used downed tree limbs to build a lean-to. He threw smaller sticks on top of the tree limbs and then piled dead branches and dirt on top of that. By the time he finished, it was impossible to tell that his shelter was not part of the landscape. He set up his tent underneath the lean-to.

*Pine Ridge Reservation, South Dakota: Sunday, June 12*

When Nathan woke up, he thought about the fact that this was going to be a much different Sunday than the one he had been dreaming about for the past two years. Every time he had a good experience on his mission, he wondered if it would be one of the stories he would tell when he spoke in sacrament meeting in his own ward. He had some of the same kinds of experiences he had heard missionaries tell about since he was a child—faith promoting and emotional—about people who came to know that the Book of Mormon was true and then joined the Church. The big difference was that these were his stories; he had lived them.

Two days before he was to leave Seattle, he had written notes for the talk he would give. Now he wondered if, by the time he got home, his mission would be entirely overshadowed by what had happened since then.

He knew he was putting his parents through a difficult time. He hoped Trish had talked to them by now. He wished he could just call and tell them what had happened, but he didn't want to put them in danger. He would just have to hope they could hold on until he was able to get home.

He was all alone now. The only one he could go to for help was God. He got dressed and then walked a little way out of camp and found a spot sheltered by a large boulder. He knelt down and closed his eyes. "Father in Heaven . . . " he began.

▼ ▼ ▼

*Rexburg, Idaho: Sunday, June 12*

Meetings at the Rexburg Sixth Ward began at one o'clock. "You're not getting ready?" Boyd asked his wife at eleven-thirty.

"I'm not going."

"Why not?"

"I can't face everyone asking where Nathan is. What do I say when they ask me about him?"

"We should go to church," Boyd said.

"Why?"

"So we can pray for him."

"I've been praying since Thursday. If that's not good enough, then I don't think saying a prayer at church is going to do it either."

"Nathan would want us to go to church."

"I'm sorry, Boyd, but I just can't go. I'm too emotional. I start crying for no reason. You go on without me."

At a quarter to twelve, Preston Sherman, their home teacher, dropped by. Boyd answered the door. Preston was a retired potato farmer who'd moved to Rexburg after selling his farm. He was a big, slow-talking man with a voice that sounded like it was coming from a cave.

"The wife thought you might like this," he said, handing Boyd a casserole.

"There's no reason . . . we're perfectly able . . . "

"I know." Preston smiled. "I tried to talk her out of it, but you know how these women are."

"We don't know where Nathan is," Boyd said.

"I heard that this morning. I was sorry to hear it. Well, I'm sure he'll show up. He's like you, practically indestructible."

"Elaine's taking it pretty hard."

"You want me to help you give her a blessing?" Preston asked.

"Let me go ask her."

A few minutes later Elaine came out of the bedroom into the living room, still in a robe. The Shermans and Williamses had been good friends for a long time. "Now, Preston," she said, "don't you go around telling everybody you saw me in a robe this late in the day."

"I promise I won't."

"Thank you for coming," she said.

"No problem."

"I guess we need you now."

"I'll do the best I can—you know that."

Boyd moved one of the dining-room chairs into the center of the living room. Elaine sat down and closed her eyes and waited for the words that would give her comfort. The two men gently laid their huge hands on her head, and Preston began to speak.

Later that day she and Boyd went to church. Elaine found it comforting to be with her friends. They didn't have any answers, but they showed her they cared with their hugs.

▼ ▼ ▼

*Pine Ridge Reservation: June 13–20*

On his mission Nathan had been the master of time management. And so, even alone in a tent with nothing to do and nobody to talk to during the day, on Monday he set up a daily schedule.

The first thing he did every morning was get cleaned up. That was a more time-consuming operation than it had been on his mission. He learned to take a bath with only a washcloth and a small amount of water. His breakfast mostly consisted of powdered oatmeal prepared with water.

After breakfast he read from the Book of Mormon. Because it was the only book he had in camp, he usually read it for two or three hours a day.

The first few days he spent hours on a butte watching the road for cars, but few passed by; he soon realized that because it was a gravel road, he would be able to hear any approaching vehicle. It was not that he and Jessica had forgotten that Steiger was looking for them, but as time passed they began to feel as if they had been cut off from the rest of the world. On some days not a single car passed down the gravel road that was the only connecting link to the outside. In all the time he was there, he saw only one small plane fly directly overhead.

Near dusk, when he would be least likely to be spotted, he walked or ran among the scrub pines and rolling hills in the area.

He went over and over in his mind what else he should be doing to protect himself and Jessica. He had her talk to people who worked at the gas station and stores and ask them to tell her if anybody came around asking where she lived. Steiger couldn't find them unless someone showed him. And if he came, he'd come in a car. And if he came in a car, Nathan would hear him.

Nathan realized they were the most vulnerable when Jessica was working. Steiger could get to her then. And if he had her, he might use her as a hostage to get to Nathan. He asked her to stop working, but she refused, telling him that he was becoming paranoid.

It was at night, from two in the morning until sunrise, that Nathan's fears got the upper hand. Some nights he'd wake up suddenly. Maybe it was a small animal outside the tent looking for something to eat or a sudden gust of wind that would make a sound. Whatever it was, he'd sit up and grab the gun. He'd find himself imagining the sound of approaching footsteps, but then it would be quiet again. He'd get up and get dressed and walk down the hill until he was close to the house where Jessica and her grandmother were sleeping. Then he'd sit there keeping guard over the house until sunrise, when he'd go back to bed.

The most important part of his day was when Jessica came to see him. She usually came sometime around eleven at night. She didn't come earlier because she was worried her grandmother might see her and wonder what she was up to. And so she came late. Because Nathan was used to mission hours, he would have preferred her to come earlier, but he never said anything to her. He was lonesome and grateful she came at all.

Since he was staying in the wooded hills only a few hundred yards above where she and her grandmother lived, Jessica could have walked. But usually she drove the Jimmy because of the necessity of hauling water. He told her the Jimmy was hers to keep but asked her to see if she could somehow get South Dakota plates without registering it. The next night when she came, the Washington plates had been removed and South Dakota plates were on the vehicle. She had borrowed the plates from a friend whose car didn't work anymore. Each time she came she would bring three full water containers and he'd give her three empties for her to fill up the next time.

Because she was the only person Nathan saw, his day was centered in her visits. On the second night she came, she said, "You know, this is a lot like taking care of a pet. I make sure you have plenty of water and food, and I pet you on the head a couple of times. I don't suppose you could start running out to greet me on all fours with your tail wagging and your tongue hanging out of your mouth?"

"Ruff, ruff," he answered.

"Good dog."

"You want me to do tricks for you?" he asked.

"What can you do?"

Nathan became serious. "Roll over and play dead."

"That's one trick I never want to see you do." She looked at the star-strewn sky. "I couldn't sleep last night," she said, "because I kept thinking about you."

"What about?"

"I have great respect for you," she said.

"Why?"

"Because you live by a code of conduct. In that way you're

like our Lakota leaders of long ago—Red Cloud, Sitting Bull, Crazy Horse. For us these men were like your Thomas Jefferson, George Washington, and Abraham Lincoln." She pulled a bent piece of paper from a billfold. "You need to hear this. I've kept it since I first read it in a newspaper. It was said by Chief Sitting Bull." She began to read. "'They say that I am a bad Indian. What white man has ever seen me drunk? Who has ever come to me hungry and unfed? Who has ever seen me beat my wives or abuse my children? . . . Is it wicked for me because my skin is red? Because I am Sioux; because I was born where my father lived; because I would die for my people and my country?'"

"That's good. I can see why you keep it."

"We had strong leaders then. And then for a while we didn't seem to have any. But now I think those days are coming back. More than anything, I want to be strong so I can help the younger ones coming along."

"You *are* strong," he said.

"I hope I am. It's what I want most of all. That's why I work so hard in school. If you could see the way I am at the School of Mines working with our freshmen, you'd be proud of me."

"I *am* proud of you. What you're doing is really important."

"It's becoming the most important thing in my life. Sometimes I think I can hear my ancestors telling me to keep going and not give up. Things are happening now among my people, exciting things. We are like a sleeping giant waking up. We are the one group of people who have always had great respect for the earth. The world needs that now. The nations of the world have done so much damage to this planet. We can help. I know we can. I want to be a part of the destiny I see for my people."

"You will be," he said.

"You and I are a lot alike in some ways. What makes you strong?"

"I can tell you, but it might take a few days. Is that all right with you?"

"Yes, while you're here I want to learn as much as I can from you."

"There's plenty I can learn from you, too," he said.

"Do you really believe that, or are you just saying it?"

"After spending time with you, I believe it."

"What do you think you can learn from me?" she asked.

"I can come to value your heritage."

"I hope that happens. I'll be glad to teach you what I know. How are you going to teach me what you want me to learn?"

"I'd like us to read the Book of Mormon together for maybe half an hour every night when you come. Is that okay?"

"I'm not looking for a church to join—but I'll read your book with you if you think it will help."

Nathan smiled. "I think it will."

The next night when she came, they sat next to each other in the tent with a Coleman lantern hanging above them. Nathan offered a prayer and then they began to read. He would read a page out loud and then hand the book for her to read the next page.

He couldn't help but wonder if any of her Lamanite ancestors were watching as he and Jessica read to each other.

# CHAPTER EIGHT

*Rexburg, Idaho: June 12–19*

BECAUSE OF WHAT TRISH HAD SAID, Elaine had to face the possibility that her son had run off with a young woman. But even if he had, why hadn't he called them directly instead of going through Trish? What had happened to make him run away from his family and from the way he'd been taught all his life?

No matter what she was doing around the house, her thoughts were constantly on Nathan. Her mind wouldn't let go of it. She found herself imagining all sorts of terrible possibilities of what might have happened. Had he somehow become involved with a girl? But how could that be if his companion didn't know anything about it? Maybe he'd sneaked out at night while his companion was sleeping. Was the girl pregnant? Was that why he couldn't face coming home? The variations ran on endlessly through her mind. With each scenario she wanted to tell him, "We can work it out. Whatever's happened, we can work it out. Just come home. We'll work it out. Please, just come home."

Boyd Williams poured his energy into trying to discover the facts. Every attempt he made to find out details of Flight 832 ended in vague answers and guarded phrases. One person finally admitted over the phone, "We have been told not to say anything about what happened."

"Who told you that?"

"Security."

"Can you give me a name of someone I can talk to?"

"No, I'm sorry, I can't."

On Tuesday, June 14, Nathan's mission president called to say that a man from the Church security office would be in Seattle on Thursday to investigate Nathan's disappearance. "Perhaps you'd like to be here when he comes," he told Boyd. "You're welcome to stay at the mission home with us."

The next day Boyd turned the farm chores over to a hired hand and drove to Seattle.

▼ ▼ ▼

*Seattle, Washington: Thursday, June 16*

James Doyle from the Church security office was a retired FBI agent who preferred to work behind the scenes without calling attention to himself. He looked more like an accountant than someone with experience in dealing with crime.

"I've arranged an interview with one of the flight attendants who was on the plane your son was on before his flight was cancelled," he told Boyd just after they met. "She gets in from a flight tonight at nine. We'll be meeting her in the restaurant at the hotel where she'll be staying."

Boyd spent the day with the mission president and James Doyle. They talked with members and missionaries who had known Nathan. At the end of the day, all they had learned was how effective his son had been as a missionary.

The first thing Doyle did when they met with the flight attendant was to show her a picture of Nathan. "Do you recognize him?"

"Yes, of course."

"Did anything unusual happen when Nathan was on the plane—before the plane had mechanical problems?" Boyd asked.

"They haven't told you anything?" she asked Boyd.

"No."

"Oh. I thought they would have."

"What happened?" Boyd asked.

"I saw him leave the plane with another man. Your son had a

gun in his hand. In the aisle, next to the row where he was supposed to be sitting, we found an FBI agent who was unconscious. He'd been hit over the head . . . with a gun, I guess, although I suppose it could've been anything."

Boyd couldn't believe it. "You saw Nathan leave the plane with another man? And with a gun in his hand?"

She looked at the picture again. "Yes, he's the one I saw, all right."

"And then what happened?" Doyle asked.

"The police and FBI came and searched the plane and went through everybody's luggage, and then they talked to every passenger individually. The FBI agent made everyone promise not to say anything about what had happened, but I thought they would have told the family."

▼ ▼ ▼

Because Doyle had met Jack Donovan once before when he worked for the FBI, he was able to make an appointment for him and Boyd to meet with Donovan the next day. Boyd thought the office was too fancy for any policeman he'd ever known—dark mahogany paneling, several paintings of whales on the walls, and a large, expensive-looking desk. Prominent in the room was a top-of-the-line computer on the desk.

"Please sit down," Donovan said. "Can I get either of you anything to drink? Coffee, tea, soft drink?"

"I didn't come all this way because I was thirsty," Boyd said.

"No, of course not." Donovan pointed to the picture of his family on his desk. "I'm a father too—we have two children. This is my oldest daughter, Elizabeth. She just graduated from Brown University. And this is my son, Todd. He'll be a sophomore at Harvard in the fall. As one father to another, let me assure you I want to find your son as much as you do."

"We have been told that Nathan Williams left the plane with a gun in his hand, and that he left with another man," Doyle said. "Do you know the name of the man?"

"Yes, I do. His name was Gibbs. He was one of our agents. Unfortunately, we've discovered he was taking money from drug dealers. We were about to arrest him. I suspect what happened was that when one of our officers entered the plane, Gibbs was desperate enough to offer Nathan Williams a lot of money to help him—perhaps several hundred thousand dollars. Few young men could resist that kind of an offer."

Boyd jumped up out of his seat. "Are you saying my son took money to help a drug dealer?"

Donovan sat calmly in his big swivel chair and spoke in a quiet voice. "That's the way it looks to us right now. When your son left the plane with Gibbs, our agent had been knocked unconscious and your son was carrying our agent's gun. I know this must be a shock to you . . . "

"My son would never do that."

"Everyone has a price, Mr. Williams. Everyone." Donovan decided to end the discussion. "I'm afraid I'll have to ask you both to leave now. I have an important meeting. I'm chairing a task force assigned to recommend steps that are needed to reduce crime in Seattle."

Boyd was ready to grab Donovan, but one look at Doyle calmed him from doing anything drastic.

Boyd and Doyle walked silently to their car in the parking lot. "You go home, Brother Williams," Doyle said. "Let me see what I can find out. I'll let you know what I turn up."

▼ ▼ ▼

*Pine Ridge Reservation: Tuesday, June 14*

On Tuesday night Nathan had a nightmare in which he watched Steiger beating Jessica. In his dream he tried to make Steiger stop hurting her, but his blows were like a small child against an adult, and did nothing but cause Steiger to laugh. He tried to shoot Steiger, but his gun wouldn't work. He pulled the trigger again, and the gun fell apart into pieces, which landed on the floor and clattered away in all directions.

When he woke up, his heart was racing and he was drenched with sweat. There was no one to talk to, no one to ease his pain and soothe his fears. He closed his eyes and fought against the feeling of helplessness that threatened to engulf him.

He stood up and walked to a lookout to see if there were any cars on the road below. There was no traffic of any kind. When morning came, he stayed there and read his Book of Mormon. After a few minutes he started to read what Moroni had written at the beginning of his years of isolation. "My father hath been slain in battle, and all my kinsfolk, and I have not friends nor whither to go; and how long the Lord will suffer that I may live I know not."

Moroni had also been alone, hiding from his enemies and not knowing how much longer he would live. Nathan had that much in common with him.

Around eight in the morning he returned to his tent and slept until noon.

*Pine Ridge Reservation: Wednesday, June 15*

On Wednesday night Nathan asked Jessica to bring him an empty five-gallon can, a hacksaw, and a cake mix. On Thursday she brought them. On Friday he made a reflecting oven.

When she came on Saturday night, he asked her if she'd like a piece of cake. She took a bite. "This is really good."

He smiled. "Yeah, I know. I'm thinking of starting a bakery."

"I'm impressed," she said.

"It'd be better with frosting, but I didn't know how to do that."

"You always keep busy, don't you. I mean, every day you do something."

"It's just the way I was brought up," he said. "I remember one time when I was working during potato harvest and some of the equipment broke down. I must have been only eleven or twelve. I sat down to rest, and my dad came over to me and said, 'Nathan, I don't think you understand why we're out here. It's not just to put in our time. We're here to do a job. You should be looking around all the time for things that need to be done. I shouldn't have to tell you everything.' And then he gave me about three or four jobs I could have been doing instead of just sitting around. That's where I learned it from—from my dad."

"I never really knew my dad, at least not that way. But my grandma's that way. She's the good example in my life."

"Not your mom?"

"No. My mom is a little on the wild side. She's in Denver now."

"What about your dad?"

"I haven't heard from him in years. My grandmother raised me from the time I was four. She's the one who taught me to get as much education as I can. She says that the warriors of today are the ones who get a good education. She's right, of course, but in a way it's funny because she had a real bad experience in school when she was little. When she was eight years old the government took her away from her family and put her into a boarding school where they'd punish her if she talked Lakota, and they cut her hair and made her wear starched uniforms, and she never got to see her mom or dad or her younger brothers and sisters. They wanted to turn them into whites, but it never worked.

"Being Lakota is more than what you wear or how you talk. The sad thing, though, is that where other kids can remember family, all she has is a blank. But the one thing it did for her was give her a love for books and reading. Everything else about it was bad—very bad. She doesn't talk about it much, but when she does, she cries."

"Why did the government do that?" he asked.

"Because they thought of us as savages. They were trying to save the children, I guess. The only thing we needed saving from was them. We had a culture of our own. We didn't need what they had. We had lived on the plains for hundreds of years. We could have stayed there for hundreds of years more, but they would have none of it. They killed the buffalo, and that took away our source of food. Then they forced us onto some of the worst land they could find and gave us food we couldn't stand, and they gave us blankets infected with smallpox, and they took away our pride and our lives and our dignity. But we're coming back now, and nothing they can do will stop us."

"What do you want for your people?" he asked.

"The same thing you take for granted: we want to have a say in what happens to us."

▼ ▼ ▼

*Sunday, June 19*

Nathan was excited that he had only one more week to go. The next Sunday issue of the paper should say "only one puppy left." He could be on his way home the next day. Just one more week.

*June 20–22*

Nathan and Jessica continued to read from the Book of Mormon in his tent. It wasn't the best arrangement. Even after a few minutes, it became uncomfortable for them to sit up with no backrest.

On Wednesday night, she said, "I know a place we can go where we'd be more comfortable."

"Where?"

"The teacher's lounge at Little Wound School. I've got a key to the building. There's nobody there at night. And even if anybody comes, I'm a custodian and sometimes custodians work at night, so nobody will think anything of it."

"Okay, let's do it."

The first thing Jessica showed Nathan once they got inside Little Wound School was the gym where the walls were covered with murals of Native American themes. "This is where I spent most of my time while I was growing up," she said. "They left the building open nights for people to play basketball."

They walked up a ramp to the second floor.

"I loved this school when I was going to it, and I love it now," she said, turning toward Nathan. "Someday I want to teach here part-time."

"I really admire you for wanting to help."

"You'd be the same as me if you'd been born an Indian."

"I hope I would."

"You would. I'm sure of it."

She turned on the light in the teachers' lounge. The room had no outside windows, so they would not be seen from the street.

They sat across from each other at a long table. After he offered a prayer, they began to read again.

That night, she read from chapter 15 of First Nephi: " ' . . . and many generations after the Messiah shall be manifested in body unto the children of men, then shall the fulness of the gospel of the Messiah come unto the Gentiles, and from the Gentiles unto the remnant of our seed.' "

"Whenever it says 'remnant of our seed' in the Book of Mormon, it's talking about Indians," Nathan explained. "Keep reading."

She continued. " 'And at that day shall the remnant of our seed know that they are of the house of Israel, and that they are the covenant people of the Lord; and then shall they know and come to the knowledge of their forefathers, and also to the knowledge of the gospel of their Redeemer, which was ministered unto their fathers by him.' " She stopped again. "What does that mean?"

"Jesus Christ, right after he was resurrected, came to this continent and taught your ancestors."

"Why haven't you told me this before now?" she asked.

"I was hoping I could get to it while we were on the plane, but then we were interrupted by Steiger. You say you want to be strong. Well, there are some strong leaders of your people you can read about in this book. They're my heroes. I hope they'll become yours too."

*Rexburg, Idaho: Wednesday, June 22*

James Doyle of Church Security showed up unexpectedly just before ten-thirty at night. "I'm sorry it's so late."

"No, it's fine, come in," Boyd Williams said.

"I just thought I'd better check in with you."

"Elaine, this is Mister Doyle. He works for Church Security."

"I'm glad to meet you," Elaine said. "Can I get you something?"

"No, thanks. I can't stay. I spent yesterday in Seattle talking to a few people. I don't have anything definite yet. But something's not right. Unless you hear from me otherwise, don't trust Donovan."

"Why not?" Boyd asked.

"I can't tell you anything specific right now. I need to make some quiet inquiries of some friends of mine who work at FBI headquarters in D.C. to see what else I can find out."

"You think Donovan might have something to do with our son's disappearance?" Boyd asked.

"To tell you the truth, I don't know. Have you heard anything at all from your son since we talked last?"

Elaine tried to decide what to say. Nathan had told Trish to tell his parents not to tell anyone he had called. Besides, if they couldn't trust the FBI, who could they trust? How did they know this man Doyle really worked for Church Security anyway?

"No," Elaine said quickly. "We haven't heard a thing."

▼ ▼ ▼

*Pine Ridge Reservation: Thursday, June 23*

This night when Jessica came to see Nathan, she seemed angry at him. "I don't want to read any more from your book," she said. "I think it's time for me to show *you* a few things."

They got into the Jimmy, and she drove. They rode in near silence for several minutes until he finally asked what was wrong.

"You think you know what it's like for me here, but you don't know a thing. What makes you think you can tell me about my heritage? People like you are so ignorant. You think you know what's wrong with us. You think you can fix us, don't you? Everyone thinks that. Everyone wants to do something about the 'Indian problem.' What makes you think there's a problem anyway? Because we're not like whites? As if that were some great recommendation. We don't want to be like you!"

"What brought this on?"

"I just realized something. You're trying to turn me into an apple, aren't you."

"What's an apple?"

"Red on the outside but white on the inside."

In about half an hour she pulled over to a small, deserted

graveyard and turned the engine off. "This is Wounded Knee," she said. "Do you know anything about what happened here?"

"No."

"I didn't think you would. It's not something they teach in history classes. Well, you need to know. In 1891, U.S. soldiers opened fire on unarmed Indian men, women, and children. They killed over two hundred people for no reason. It was the end of our pride as a people, and it was the beginning of reservation handouts. Even little babies were shot."

"How did it start?"

"Someone fired a shot. Nobody knows who. After that, all the soldiers started firing at anything that moved—little boys and girls, old women, old men, young men, pregnant women—all shot down. The Indian leader, Big Foot, was shot. They left him on the ground. That night it got very cold, and he froze. They took a picture of him like this—his hand up, as if trying to get up."

At first Nathan wasn't sure what he was supposed to say or why she had brought him here. "I'm sorry it happened," he said, as they walked slowly around the cemetery.

"If you'd been a soldier in that company and I'd been living then, you might have shot me as I tried to escape."

"I would never have done that."

"You can't say what you would have done if you'd lived then. Nobody can."

"We're not living then—we're living now."

"It's not that much different now. Sometimes when I come here I imagine I can hear their voices."

"Their voices from the dust?"

"Yes. Why did you say that?"

"Because that's what the Book of Mormon is—the written words of a nation of people who were destroyed by war, crying from the dust . . . to you."

"Not to me, to you," she said.

"No, to you. It was written for you and your people."

"There're a lot of things I don't like about that book," she went on.

"What?"

"I don't appreciate it saying that dark skin was a curse given by God. Do you think I'm cursed because I have a dark skin?"

"No, not at all."

"Answer me this, and be honest. Do you think I'm less of a person because my skin is darker than yours?"

"No."

"Are you sure?"

"God doesn't care what the color of a person's skin is. What he cares about is if they keep his commandments."

"There's something I've got to tell you, and this is as good a place as any to tell you, next to the graves of my people who were killed. I know you want me to join your church, but you need to know that my destiny will always be with my people. You went on a mission. Well, I have a mission too. My mission is with the Lakota nation."

"I think that's great."

"Let me tell you what I'm really thinking. I think the Mormon church is just another white man's religion," she said.

"It may have been once, but it isn't that way anymore. In just a few years whites will be in the minority as members of the Church. In Mexico alone there're nearly a million Mormons. Hispanics and Indians by the thousands are joining in South America."

"Why are they doing that?"

"Because they know that it's true. Let me ask you a question— when you've read the Book of Mormon, have you had a feeling in your heart that it's from God?"

She shook her head. "No, not at all. Sorry."

"Jessica, I know you've felt something. Don't deny it."

"If you're such a big expert on my feelings, you tell me what I felt."

"You had a feeling that you've never had before. It was a warm, comforting feeling. But then it scared you because it meant that you needed to change the way you live."

"Why can't you get it into your head that you don't know how I feel!" She turned and walked away. He started toward her, but she shook her head and waved him back. He went to the Jimmy and waited.

She stayed alone in the dark for several minutes. When she finally did come back, she got in the driver's seat. She started the engine and put it in gear. Slowly they pulled away.

"Can I read you something from the Book of Mormon?" he asked.

"Would you please just give this up? You make me so mad sometimes."

"Just one thing."

She sighed. "Oh, all right, but this is the last time you ever read to me from that book."

He turned on the dome light and explained, "These are the last words that Mormon wrote. He was the one who abridged the records. He spent the last years of his life trying to fight your ancestors, but it was no use. By this time his people were more wicked than your ancestors. Just before being killed in battle, he wrote this to his former enemies, but not to them as much as to future generations of your people. Jessica, he wrote this to you."

She rolled her eyes. "Is this going to take very long?" she asked.

"No, not long." He started reading: "'And now, behold, I would speak somewhat unto the remnant of this people who are spared, if it so be that God may give unto them my words, that they may know of the things of their fathers; yea, I speak unto you, ye remnant of the house of Israel; and these are the words which I speak.'"

He stopped. "Like I said before, whenever it talks about 'remnant' of this people, it's referring to Indians. So you really can treat this as if he wrote it just for you, okay?"

"Look, just get this over with."

He began reading again. "'Know ye that ye are of the house of Israel. Know ye that ye must come unto repentance, or ye cannot be saved. . . . Know ye that ye must come to the knowledge of your fathers, and repent of all your sins and iniquities, and believe in Jesus Christ, that he is the Son of God, and that he was slain by the Jews, and by the power of the Father he hath risen again, whereby he hath gained the victory over the grave; and also in him is the sting of death swallowed up. And he bringeth to pass the resurrection of the dead, whereby men must be raised to stand before his judgment-seat. And he hath brought to pass the redemption of the world, whereby he that is found guiltless before him at the judgment day hath it given unto him to dwell in the presence of God in his kingdom, to sing ceaseless praises with the choirs above, unto the Father, and unto the Son, and unto the Holy Ghost, which are one God, in a state of happiness which hath no end.'"

He looked at her, trying to gauge how much more she would let him say, then commented, "All those people who were killed at Wounded Knee will be resurrected someday. They'll be alive again on this earth, and they'll never die. Right after they died, they were taught. They've had the opportunity to accept the message or reject it, just as you're having that same opportunity now. Some of them have accepted it, and they're waiting for someone like you to be baptized for them in one of our temples."

"All of them have been taught?"

"Yes, all of them. Listen to this next part. This is for you." He continued reading. "'Therefore repent, and be baptized in the name of Jesus, and lay hold upon the gospel of Christ, which shall be set before you, not only in this record but also in the record which shall come unto the Gentiles from the Jews, which record shall come from the Gentiles unto you. For behold, this is written for the intent that ye may believe that; and if ye believe that ye will believe this also; and if ye believe this ye will know concerning your fathers, and also the marvelous works which were wrought by the power of God among them. And ye will also know that ye are a remnant of the seed of Jacob; therefore ye are numbered among the people of the first covenant; and, if it so be that ye believe in Christ, and are baptized, first with water, and then with fire and with the Holy Ghost, following the example of our Savior, according to that which he hath commanded us, it shall be well with you in the day of judgment. Amen.'"

"Are you done?"

"I'm done."

"Good. I wish we'd never started this."

"Why do you wish that?"

She wouldn't answer.

"You *have* felt something, haven't you?" he asked.

Still no answer.

"What are you going to do about it?"

"Don't talk to me about it anymore. I'm serious, Nathan."

"All right, I won't."

She let out a sigh of relief. "Finally."

# CHAPTER NINE

*Pine Ridge Reservation: Friday, June 24*

JESSICA CAME TO SEE HIM EARLY IN THE MORNING on her way to work. It was as if her anger of the night before had never happened. "Hey, sleepyhead, time to get up," she said. "Can I come in?"

"Okay."

She stuck her head inside the tent. "When I was getting ready this morning, I thought of a way you can get home a day early. Tomorrow night we could drive to Rapid City and wait for them to deliver the *Denver Post* to a store like 7-Eleven. Then you could catch an early flight to Salt Lake City on Sunday and be back in Idaho by early afternoon."

"Great idea! I can hardly wait to get home and see my family again. I might even be able to go to church with them Sunday, because we have church in the afternoon."

"That means tonight is our last night here together. I think we need to celebrate getting through this. You want to go dancing?"

"Where would we go?"

"Chadron, Nebraska. It's just over the state line. I was going to take you to a bar, but I knew you'd never go for that. So I've been asking around and found out there's a church there that has a dance once a month. We'll have a good time. And we could eat out, too. There's a great place to eat in Chadron. How would you like a big juicy steak dinner, a baked potato with sour cream, some hot rolls just out of the oven, corn on the cob, and home-made banana cream pie?"

"That sounds a lot better than the powdered oatmeal I've been eating. But what if someone recognizes me?"

"What's there to recognize? You don't even look like you did when you were on your mission. In fact, with that tan, you look a little bit like a 'Skin. C'mon, Nathan, don't be such a deadhead. Take me dancing."

They left at six-thirty. Jessica drove because she knew the roads. It was the first time he'd seen her wearing makeup. The effect was stunning.

The cafe was crowded, and they had to wait for a vacant table. Nathan gave his name to the hostess as Matt White Cloud.

After half an hour it seemed to him that some people who had come in after them were seated before they were. He went up to the hostess and complained. She said, "Well, aren't we uppity tonight?" and brushed by him. He wasn't going to let her get away with that. He followed her into the kitchen. "What do you want?" she asked.

"I want us to be the next ones seated."

"And if you're not?"

"I'll see a lawyer in the morning."

The hostess stared at him. He stared back then lifted up his shirt sleeve so she could see the distinctive line between tan and white.

Her mood changed immediately. "Sorry. For a minute there, I thought you were an Indian. Yes, of course, you'll be the next one. Sorry for the inconvenience."

Five minutes later they were seated. Jessica asked him how he'd done it, but he was too ashamed to tell her that the color of his skin under his shirt had done what his tan and her complexion could not do.

After they ordered, their waitress, who must not have got the word about them, said, "This is going to cost you more than twenty dollars. You got that much?" She talked down to them as though they were children.

Nathan pulled out two twenty-dollar bills and laid them on

the table. "One of these is for you if you can serve us without talking down to us."

"I guess for twenty dollars I can do that."

"Do it then."

The waitress left.

"Do you have to put up with this all the time?" he asked.

"No, not all the time. Some people don't seem to notice the color of my skin. Others can't see much else. I try not to let it bother me."

The food was excellent. By the time they finished eating, the cafe wasn't as crowded, and they had some time to relax and enjoy themselves without worrying what people thought.

At the dance, which was held at a community church, they stood in line and paid their money, but Nathan noticed a few people staring at them.

Nathan had never been much for dancing. Not only that, but they didn't feel very welcome there either. So for the first half hour all they did was stand in a corner and watch. Then they drifted away from the dance floor until they found themselves out in the hall. The main hallway was filled with a steady stream of people because that was where the rest rooms were, but farther down the hall and around the corner, they found an empty classroom set up for young children.

They stepped inside. Jessica came in close to him and put her head on his shoulder, and they began to rock slowly back and forth in time to the music. This was the first time he had been this close to a girl in two years.

"Maybe we should take a break or something," he said after a minute.

"What for?"

"I just got back from a mission."

"Poor baby," she teased.

"I'm serious. I'm just not used to this."

"Okay. Let's take a break."

They played a game of beanbag toss that was set up for the children. But then, fifteen minutes later, she told him he had to dance with her when the band began playing one of her favorite songs. She snuggled close to him. As he held her in his arms, he lightly ran his fingers through her hair. It was smooth and straight and very dark.

"Hey, who's messing with my hair?" she whispered.

"I am."

"Good—I was hoping it was you."

He remembered when he had first seen her on the plane, how dark he thought she looked, but now she looked normal and everyone else at the dance looked pale.

They might have stayed in the children's classroom until the dance was over, but the wife of the minister found them there. "What are you doing here?" she demanded.

"We're just dancing."

Nathan watched as she looked around the room with her eyes. He wondered if she thought they had stolen something. "This is a classroom for children, not a dance floor," she said. "If you want to dance, you should go in where everyone else is."

"People stare at us," Nathan explained.

"Don't be silly. Nobody is staring at you."

Jessica had a point to prove to Nathan. "So, you think we're being overly sensitive?"

"Yes, that's exactly what I think."

The woman was standing guard, waiting for Nathan and Jessica to leave the room. Nathan couldn't let it go at that. "Are you the minister's wife?" he asked.

"Yes, I am."

Nathan guessed that she and her husband had given everything they had to this little church and that every chair and blackboard was part of their life. Nathan had met a couple of ministers like that while on his mission, and he had learned to respect them greatly. He saw them as good people who gave everything they had for their beliefs. "Thank you for opening up your church for this dance," he told the woman.

Her lips opened slightly, and she looked surprised. "We've been holding these dances once a month for two years. You're the only one who's ever thanked us."

"You and your husband are doing a great job here. I mean it. Keep it up, okay?"

"If you want to stay here, I suppose it'll be all right. It's just that I worry so."

"Thank you, but we need to be starting back," Nathan said.

"I'm sorry if I sounded mean. We're so strapped for funds here to keep it all going. Sometimes after a dance things turn up missing. My husband doesn't notice it, but I do. We've lost more than he'll ever admit to." She walked with them to the door. "Please, come back anytime. For Sunday services if you'd like. You'll always be welcome here."

"Thank you," Jessica said. As they walked out to the Jimmy, she commented to Nathan, "She's really nice."

"Yeah, she is."

"I want you to drive," she said.

"I'm not sure I know the way."

"I'll tell you which way to go."

"Why do you want me to drive?"

"Because I want to fall asleep in your arms, and I think this is about the only way that's ever going to happen to us."

With bucket seats and a rise down the middle for the transmission, getting close was not easy. Finally they worked it out; he slid clear to the left side, and they both just managed to sit in the driver's seat.

"One of us is taking up too much room," she teased.

"Oh yeah? Well, it's not me."

She gave him a tap in the rib cage. "Oh, is that right?"

"Don't bother the driver," he said, reminding himself of his dad when they went on long family vacations.

She kept rearranging herself until finally she was snuggled up against him with her head on his shoulder. He put his right arm around her to keep her close.

Minutes of silence drifted by, and then she looked up at him and asked, "You like me a lot, don't you?"

"Yes, more than any girl I've ever known."

"I like you too, Nathan. You're my best friend right now. I feel really good when I'm with you."

"I do too."

"I'm going to miss you when you leave."

"I'll miss you too."

"You know you're one of my heroes, don't you?" she asked.

"I didn't know that."

"Well, you are."

"Letting me stay here is saving my life," he said.

"We're both Lifesavers," she said. "What kind do you want to be, cherry or lime?"

"Whatever kind you are."

"I'm cherry 'cause they're red."

"Then that's what I'll be."

"Two cherry Lifesavers, that's what we are," she said, her voice trailing off.

She fell asleep under his arm. At the next turnoff, though, he had to wake her to find out which way to go.

They got home around two in the morning. He stopped the Jimmy and got out far enough from her grandmother's house that she wouldn't see him even if she were awake. He watched Jessica drive off, and then he walked up the hill to his tent and crawled into his sleeping bag and went to sleep.

▼ ▼ ▼

*Saturday, June 25*

Because this was his last day on the reservation, he saw no reason to get up at any particular time, so he slept in until eleven o'clock.

Somewhere between sleep and consciousness, he had a dream. He was riding a horse through the woods. It was hundreds of years ago. He wasn't sure why he was in the woods—maybe because he was a trapper. He was following a trail. He came around a bend and there was Jessica, dressed in buckskin. She didn't run away when she saw him. He got off his horse and walked up to her. They looked into each other's eyes and then he kissed her. He got on his horse and motioned for her to get up behind him. He lifted her up, and she wrapped both arms around his waist and rested her head on his back. Together they rode away to his cabin. And she stayed with him from then on.

When he woke up, he wanted to go back to his dream. But it wouldn't come back, so he got up.

He usually knew when she was coming because he would hear the Jimmy, but that morning she walked up the hill to see him. He had been washing himself and still had his shirt off. He was shaving as she tried to sneak up behind him, but he saw her in the mirror he had hung from the branch of a tree. He smiled and turned around.

"My gosh, you are so white!" she exclaimed. "How can you stand to look like that? A 'Skin who's been dead three days looks a lot better than you do."

"Oh, is that right?" He moved ominously toward her with the shaving-cream can. "How would you like to be all white for a change? I think I can arrange it." He pointed the shaving-cream can in her direction.

"Nathan, don't, I'm serious. Don't mess with me." She backed up and then ran a short distance from him and stopped.

He ran and caught up with her. They stood there, looking at each other.

"Why don't you come and get me, Nathan?" she teased, running off again, heading straight up the hill.

He ran after her. He wanted there to be a chase, and he wanted her to giggle as he ran after her. He was having a great time, and yet the part of his mind that had made him such a good fleet coordinator on his mission wondered whether it was wise for him to be running through the woods with his shirt off, chasing a dark-eyed, beautiful girl whose long dark hair was swinging rhythmically with every step she took.

But the race was on, and there could be no turning back. Finally he caught up with her and grabbed her by the arm.

"Looks like you caught me!" she said. They were both breathing hard.

"Looks that way."

"Now you've got me, what are you going to do with me?" she teased.

It was their last day together and they were in love with each other, and after tomorrow all either of them would have of the other would be a memory. At that moment, with the sound of birds and a light morning breeze and the sun just beginning to warm the carpet of pine needles that formed the forest floor, and with her wearing a simple T-shirt and jeans and no makeup on her face, Jessica was the most beautiful girl Nathan had ever seen. If the world were to stop and if time were to freeze forever, if he only could have one moment to live over and over again, it would be that moment. It was a moment of uncertainty and doubt and unbelievable tension, anticipation, and excitement.

He wasn't sure what was about to happen. He knew he wanted to kiss her, not just once but many times. That scared him; this was new territory for him. *I need to be careful,* he thought. He knew it was only an illusion that the moment could be frozen in time. There would be a tomorrow.

Tomorrow he was going home. Tomorrow he would sit down with his stake president. Tomorrow he would look into the eyes of his mother. And tomorrow Jessica would compare what he had said about the Church's teachings to the way he had behaved. Tomorrow was on its way. He could not stop it from coming. That meant he had to be careful what he did with today. He had taught Jessica the gospel of Jesus Christ. That alone made him more responsible for his actions.

The war raging inside him felt like more than he could handle. He had to get away so he could think. He turned and walked away from her and returned to camp. He stepped inside the tent and put on his shirt. When he came out, she was waiting for him. "You gave up too soon," she said.

"You're too good a runner. The girls in Rexburg were easier to catch."

"That's because they wanted you to catch them."

"And you don't?"

She walked over to him, her head high, her eyes fixed on his, her hands down. "I'm not running from you now, Nathan. Here I am."

Her lips were slightly parted. *She wants me to kiss her,* he thought.

But he couldn't. It wasn't the right time for him. He had taught her about the Book of Mormon; he was still a missionary. He knew he owed her some kind of explanation. "I'm sorry. I'm just not ready for this."

She didn't seem offended. "Sure, no problem, I understand."

"Thanks."

"It's probably better anyway if we just stay friends."

"Probably so."

Their whole mood changed. "How does it feel for this to be your last day here?" she asked.

"It feels great. I'm anxious to see my family again. It's been a long time."

"I thought we could leave for Rapid City pretty soon. I've got some shopping to do at the mall, and then maybe we could eat out and go to a movie. I'm not sure when the *Denver Post* gets there, but I'd guess it's probably out very early in the morning. I'll just stay with you until your plane takes off. So today will be our last time to be together before you head back."

She helped him break camp. In an hour's time they had the tent and sleeping bag packed up and in the Jimmy, as well as everything else he'd used. He made one last pass to pick up any scraps of paper. Leaving the campsite better than you found it was something Scouting had taught him.

She insisted on driving. Once they got to Rapid City, she pulled into the first convenience store they came to. "I need to use the rest room," she said. "Can you get us something to eat for breakfast?"

"What do you want to eat?"

"I don't care—anything that isn't good for me."

As soon as Nathan walked into the store, the manager came over to him.

"I got ten dollars' worth of gas," Nathan said. "but we're going to get some things to eat too."

"I don't take checks," the man grumbled.

"Good, 'cause I don't have any."

Nathan walked over to the cooler to get something to drink. The manager followed him. When he picked out an orange juice for him and a Diet Pepsi for Jessica and carried them to the counter, the man followed him.

"I'm going to get a few other things," Nathan said. "But look, if you've got other things to do, I'm sure I can find what I need."

Nathan walked down to see what kind of cereal they had. The man, keeping three steps away, followed him and stood guard while he looked at the cereal. He slowly picked up a box of granola and felt the man's stare fixed on his every move.

"You got any oil?" Nathan asked.

The man talked to him as if he were stupid. "Depends what you want—cooking oil, motor oil—just tell me what you want—if you know, that is."

Nathan glanced outside. Jessica was standing by the door, watching what was going on. Then she came in. The clerk now faced a dilemma—which of them to shadow. He tried to place himself between the two of them. Jessica called out to Nathan, "We need to go."

"Not before you pay for all this," the man said.

"We don't have any money," Nathan said. "I mean, that's what you want us to say, isn't it? We just want to play the part you've created for us."

"I'm calling the cops," the manager said.

Nathan dropped a twenty-dollar bill on the counter. "Just kidding. We've got plenty of money." He flashed a roll of twenties before the man's eyes.

"What's the deal here, chief?" the man asked sarcastically. "Government checks out a little early this month, are they?"

"Do you treat your white customers this way?" Nathan asked.

"What do you think?" the owner asked.

"My friend here is white," Jessica said.

The store owner shook his head. "Half-breed maybe, but he's got some Indian in him."

"Boy, we sure can't fool you, can we?" she said.

"Not likely."

"Do you think Indians are the only ones who walk off with things without paying?" Nathan asked.

"They're responsible for a big share of what I lose every year."

"How do you know that for sure?"

"Because I get a lot of Indian business."

"Well, I'm sure we can do something about that," Nathan said emphatically.

Jessica, seeing the sweat beading up on his forehead, placed a fingertip on his lips. "Save your breath," she said softly. "Nothing you say will make any difference."

Nathan nodded, collected his change, and together they walked out of the store.

"You've never been shadowed before, have you?" she asked.

"No."

"That's because with me tagging along with you, and your great tan, you can pass as a 'Skin. Welcome to the tribe, cousin."

His chest felt like somebody was standing on it. "How often does this happen to Indians in this town?"

"Often enough. I have an aunt in Rapid City who does all her shopping by catalog because of the way she's made to feel when she walks into a store."

"It's not right."

"There are a lot of things about life that aren't right. Are you just now finding that out?"

"Yes."

She was about to pull out into the street. "You still want to go to the mall?" she asked.

"I don't want to go to any more stores."

"We could go to the School of Mines and hang around there for a while."

They went to the Native American Study Center on the third floor of the library. "Now I understand why freshmen students from the reservation need this place," he said.

"Yes, now you know. Suppose you're Indian and you've spent your whole life on the reservation, and now you're here as a freshman. Everywhere you look, you see whites. Some of them are racist, and some of them have just had a bad day. And some of them are glad you're here, but you don't know which is which. Not only that, but there are also cultural barriers. You've been taught to respect your elders and not to talk unless you're spoken to, but you don't look professors in the eye because you've been taught that's the way you show respect. But they think it's because you're not paying attention. And so it goes. At least that's the way I was my freshman year."

"You're not like that now."

"No, not now, but I was then. And even now, when I go back to the reservation, I find myself reverting back to the way I was taught. It's almost like having two personalities."

She took him into a rest room so he could look in the mirror and see why people were treating him as if he were an Indian. His face was nearly as dark as hers. He was wearing jeans and a Black Hills Powwow T-shirt she had given him. His hair was still short but a little shaggy. "None of this makes me an Indian," he said.

"No, but you were in the store with me, and there's no doubt about me. I look like an Indian."

"Why didn't that manager judge me for what I am?"

"That's what racism is. To some people, every Indian is on government welfare, and every Black likes fried chicken, and every Hispanic is a transient farm laborer."

"It's not right to treat people that way."

She knocked twice on his head. "Hello, anybody home? That's what I've been trying to tell you all this time."

"I've learned my lesson."

"Good, because this is our last day together," she said.

"I know." They looked again at their reflection in the mirror. "We look good together, don't we," Nathan said.

"Real good."

"I wonder what our kids would look like."

"Probably even better than us."

"That'd be pretty hard to do," he said, grinning.

"Are we going to stay in here all day admiring ourselves?"

"You got any better ideas?"

"Let's go to Sheridan Lake and go swimming and have a picnic."

They went to a section of the city where more Indians lived, to shop for picnic foods and buy swimming suits, towels, and sunscreen.

He drove to Sheridan Lake—a half-hour's drive from Rapid City.

"When I leave, I'm giving you the Jimmy," he said.

"Are you sure the feds will let you do that? They might want it back."

"Gibbs said I could keep whatever money I had left over."

"Well, if that's the way it works out, I'll be real glad to have it."

They were in no mood to be around people who might have racist attitudes, so they rented a pontoon boat. Jessica changed into her swimming suit in the Jimmy while Nathan hauled their picnic supplies and towels to the boat, and then he did the same while she wandered along the beach. He put on his T-shirt because he was self-conscious about being tan only on his arms, face, and neck. Then they putted slowly out to an isolated cove and anchored the boat fore and aft about ten yards from shore.

They swam for an hour and then climbed in and lay down side by side on the deck to dry off. She fell asleep. He sat up and studied her face. He remembered his reaction when he'd seen her for the very first time—how he thought her features were exaggerated. He didn't think of her in that way now. He thought she was the most beautiful girl he had ever seen.

He lay down again and wondered what it would be like to be married to her. That was something worth thinking about. He would build a house, not in town, like where his parents lived, but out on the farm. They'd have a big window in the bedroom, and he would wake up every morning next to Jessica and be able to see the green fields and her—two of the most awe-inspiring sights he could imagine.

His thoughts shifted quickly from green fields to dwell entirely on how beautiful she was as she slept next to him, just an arm's length away. Suddenly he realized he needed to get away for a while. He moved quietly to the back of the boat and slipped into the cold water. Cold water was what he needed.

He swam as hard as he could until he was tired, and then he stopped and dog-paddled. He watched a boy about twelve years old water-skiing. It reminded him of the time when he was about twelve and his uncle had tried to teach him how to water-ski. It was at a family reunion at Bear Lake on the Utah-Idaho state line. All his cousins were there from his mother's side of the family. Nathan had gotten up on the skis the first time he tried.

The only problem was that as he got up, the rushing water pulled his swimming suit down around his ankles. Embarrassed, he wasn't sure he'd be able to stand up on the skis again. He also felt as if any second he was going to crash into the water.

He had faced a difficult decision that day, whether to ski with his swimming suit around his ankles or to let go of the rope and go for modesty. Though he was far enough from shore that no one there could see him, and there were no women in the boat, he did not want to be known as the boy who had water-skied naked on Bear Lake. And even while trying to decide what to do, the thought popped into his mind that if he didn't do something soon, the name of the lake might be changed to Bare Lake. So he started laughing uncontrollably and let go of the rope. When the boat came around to get him, he was still laughing—although modest once again.

Bare Lake. He hadn't thought about that since before his mission. Just thinking about it made him miss his family even more. He was beginning to realize how much he had taken for granted growing up. He was so lucky to have grown up in a family with brothers, even older brothers who teased him unmercifully but who on the first day of high school took him around to his classes and made sure none of the seniors gave him a hard time. He also had uncles who enjoyed their high-speed boats and snowmobiles and wind surfers and who liked to backpack into the Tetons during the summer and didn't mind a boy like him tagging along.

His father had been teaching him all his life. And he had a mother who adored him. And a sister who looked up to him—or at least she did before he had left on his mission.

The swim had done him good and had allowed him to put things in perspective.

*But even so,* he thought, *I am in love with her.*

They returned the pontoon boat to the marina by seven-thirty. Before they left the lake, they took a walk into the forest.

"We call the Black Hills *Paha Sapa,*" she said. "They have always been sacred to us. We were promised this land in the Fort Laramie Treaty of 1868."

"What happened?" he asked.

"On one of his expeditions, Custer discovered gold. So then they decided they'd made a mistake, giving this land to the Indians."

"That doesn't seem fair."

"That's what we thought too. We won our lawsuit, but the government wants to pay us in money while some of us want the land. To us, land is the most important thing."

They drove back to Rapid City and went through the drive-by window at Burger King. They ate in the parking lot because Nathan was still leery of being treated like a second-class citizen.

Then they went to an area called Lakota Homes, where many Indians lived. They drove slowly through the streets, where children were still playing, though it was starting to get dark. Two boys were playing catch with a football under a streetlight. A man was working on his car under another streetlight.

Finally Jessica went to a convenience store and asked when the Sunday edition of the *Denver Post* would be in. The woman working there told them it wouldn't be in until sometime after four in the morning. Nathan looked at the clock on the wall. It was only eleven-thirty.

"Is it okay if we wait in our vehicle in your parking lot until it comes?" Nathan asked.

The clerk shrugged her shoulders. "No problem. Might help, though, if you moved back so you're not blocking my regular customers."

"Thanks a lot," Nathan said.

They moved the Jimmy to the edge of the parking lot. "When are you going to call your mom and dad?" Jessica asked.

"Soon as I find out it's okay to go home."

"That'll be some homecoming."

"Yeah, it will be."

They talked for a while and then she told him she was tired and was going to get into the backseat and go to sleep.

Time passed slowly. Nathan dozed off and on through the night. At five-fifteen a car pulled up to the newspaper racks outside the store. Nathan jumped out of the car and ran over to check the racks, only to be disappointed. The man was putting in Sunday editions of the *Rapid City Journal.*

Jessica woke up and came over to see what was going on. They sat on the curb and waited for the *Denver Post.* Fifteen minutes later the newspaper distributor drove up. Nathan paid for a copy of the *Post* before the man could put it into the rack and began rifling frantically through it until he found the want ads. He pored over it until he found the ad he was looking for. "Golden retriever puppies. Must sell. Leaving town. Two left. Phone after five or on weekends." There was a phone number given.

Jessica saw his stunned expression. "What's wrong?" she asked.

He handed her the page and she read the ad.

"What does that mean?" she asked.

He punched his fist through the page. "It means I have to wait another week, that's what it means! It means I'm not going home today after all!" He shook his head. "I can't believe it. Is this ever going to be over?"

She reached for his hand. "I'm really sorry, Nathan."

They arrived back at his campsite by seven-fifteen that morning. Nathan slammed things down on the ground as he unloaded the Jimmy.

# CHAPTER TEN

*Pine Ridge Reservation: Sunday, June 26*

IT WAS EIGHT IN THE MORNING before Nathan got his tent set up and was finally able to crawl into his sleeping bag. He was so disappointed not to be on his way home that he wished he could fall asleep and not wake up for a week.

He gave it a good try, but by three o'clock that afternoon his body had had enough sleep. But he couldn't think of any reason to get up, because no matter what he did, he was still going to be there for at least another week—or more.

The depression and anger he felt at not being able to go home helped create another problem. He found himself having to deal with what his bishop back home called "idle thoughts." He started to fantasize about what might have happened on the pontoon boat between him and Jessica if they had started kissing.

Nathan had once heard someone explain that the difference between love and lust was that love was positive and outward-focused but lust was negative and self-centered. Nathan knew he was on dangerous ground because his thoughts were both self-centered and negative.

It was a spiraling cycle. First he would let his imagination run wild until he felt guilty. And then he'd stop. But then he'd tell himself it didn't matter, and he'd start in all over again.

This was not the first time in his life he had had to deal with the kind of thoughts now invading his mind. He had learned what to do to make them go away. He needed to get up and run or at least take a long walk.

He knew that what he chose to think about was in his control. But on that morning he had hit rock bottom; he rationalized that he didn't care anymore and that nothing mattered anyhow, and, besides, he might be dead before very long.

Just before four o'clock, Jessica poked her head in the tent. She saw him still in his sleeping bag. "My gosh, Nathan, are you going to sleep all day?"

"I'm trying to, but it's not working out."

"Can I come in for a minute?"

"Yeah, sure," he said.

"You okay?"

"I've been having kind of a bad day."

"Is there anything I can do to help?" she asked.

"No. I'm okay now. I was just feeling sorry for myself, that's all."

She came inside and plopped down next to where he was lying in his sleeping bag. He sat up and used his fingers as a comb and worried about his breath.

"I've been thinking about you," she said.

He was too embarrassed to admit what he had been thinking. "What about?"

"I need to tell you something. But not here. Let's take a walk."

"Good idea."

She went outside the tent so he could get dressed. A short time later he joined her. She led him to a cliff on top of a butte, the highest point for miles around.

"You're the first person I've ever brought here," she said.

He looked around. There didn't seem to be anything particularly remarkable about the place.

"The first time I came here was when I was twelve," she began. "For me twelve was a time when I could go either of two ways. I could start down the same path some of my friends were following or I could go on a different path. My friends were all beginning to drink and spend time with older boys. My grandmother seemed to know what was happening, so she suggested I go and seek a vision. And so I did. I came up here and stayed for two days. I fasted and prayed. We call God *Wakan Tanka*. He is the Creator of all things. We also call him the Great Spirit. Sometimes we even call him Grandfather."

She looked at the scenery below. "On the first day all I could think about was how hungry I was and, in the night, how cold I was. But on the morning of the second day something happened."

"What happened?"

She dropped her gaze to avoid eye contact. "I've never told anyone this before. I had a feeling . . . that I would become a leader to my people, especially the younger ones. And because of that, I needed to live so that I could tell them to live the way I had when I was their age. From then until now, I've tried to set a good example. I've never used alcohol or drugs—and I've never spent the night with a guy. Am I embarrassing you?"

"No, not really. It's just that . . . never mind."

"There was something else. I also had the feeling that if I lived the right way, that at some time in my life, I'd be given more. When you sat down beside me on the plane, I felt that there was some reason why we were put together. But when you told me you had a message from God for me, I was shocked."

"Why?"

"It didn't make sense to me . . . because you were white. And yet I couldn't shake the feeling I had. That's why I stayed in Seattle and went to meet you at the fish market. That's why I offered to have you stay on the reservation. The only reason I asked you to pay me a thousand dollars was so I wouldn't have to explain the real reason. There have been times since then when I've decided I was mistaken about you. But now I think my feeling was valid and that God did send you to me."

Because of his thoughts earlier that day, Nathan was ashamed. What should have been an occasion for celebration now only added to his guilt.

"I think," she continued, "one reason why you weren't able to go home is because there's still more for me to learn. So I was thinking that I'd like to fast again and this time ask if I should be baptized."

"I need to fast too," he said quickly.

Later that day Jessica drove her grandmother to Wambli to visit her sister for a week. When she returned to his camp, she brought food to cook on the fire. Nathan helped her prepare what was more a ceremonial meal than anything else. After they finished eating, they knelt together and each said a prayer to begin their fast. She said her prayer in Lakota. She told him that she would not talk to him again until she ended her fast. They agreed to fast for twenty-four hours.

Early the next morning he heard someone coming. He looked outside and saw Jessica. She was wearing a white buckskin dress and moccasins. She walked slowly through his camp and up the hill and then was gone.

Nathan spent the day reading the Book of Mormon. In a long prayer he asked for forgiveness for his sins and weaknesses, especially for losing faith and hope and for allowing himself to dwell on negative thoughts the day before.

Just after sunset Jessica returned to the campsite. Her lips were parched and her skin flaked with dried-up perspiration. He offered her a drink but she refused to drink until they prayed again.

In her prayer, spoken again in Lakota, she broke down twice and had to stop. Nathan wanted to comfort her but did not because to do so might take away from what he felt was a sanctification that had come to her.

Then it was his turn to pray. He tried to be honest and not make it sound as if he was perfect just because she was listening. He asked for forgiveness and prayed that he would quit worrying so much and just put his trust in God. When he finished his prayer, he felt hopeful. He could begin again.

They were kneeling across from each other, and he handed her a metal cup of cool water. She took a small sip and handed it back to him. He took a sip and then dipped a small white cloth in the cup and reached over and gently wiped away the sweat and dried-up tear stains from her face.

With tears brimming in her eyes, she said, "I want to be baptized."

"I know," he answered.

▼ ▼ ▼

*Pine Ridge Reservation: June 28–29*

If it had been up to Jessica, they would have gone to a stream and he would have baptized her that same day. But he explained that for her name to be registered properly on the records of the Church, she needed to meet with the missionaries. Besides, even though he held the priesthood, he wasn't authorized to baptize her. The missionaries would finish teaching her about the Church, and then someone would interview her to make sure she understood what she was getting into. Then there would be a baptismal service at the church.

Every day after work that week, Jessica met with an elderly missionary couple from California. When she came home, she would go over the lesson with Nathan and persuade him to give her the next lesson so she'd know all the answers.

The baptism was scheduled for Saturday night at seven o'clock in the Pine Ridge Branch meetinghouse.

▼ ▼ ▼

*Rexburg, Idaho: Tuesday, June 28*

"I thought I'd better return this," Camille said at the door as she gave back the scrapbook about Nathan that Elaine had loaned to her just before he was scheduled to come home from his mission. "I really enjoyed looking at it. Thank you."

"Oh, thank you. Please, come in."

They sat in the living room.

"Have you heard anything from Nathan?" Camille asked.

"Yes. There's something you should know."

"What's that?" Camille asked.

"We think he's traveling with a young woman. We haven't told anyone else. But I thought you should know."

Camille looked confused. "I'm sorry. I don't understand why you thought you needed to tell me."

"You're right." Elaine's full realization of how far her hopes for Nathan and Camille had led her suddenly became clear. "Oh my . . . I'm afraid I've done something rather stupid."

"What?"

"Getting to know you over the past few months has been wonderful for me. You must know by now how much I respect and admire you. And we get along so well together. If I could, I'd claim you as my daughter. But I don't think your parents would go along with that."

Camille grinned. "Some days they would."

"Anyway, I made the mistake of thinking that you and Nathan would . . . might . . . oh gosh, this is so embarrassing to say . . . that you and Nathan might grow to like each other. I'm afraid I carried it much further in my mind than I should have. I should have known better than that by now."

"I'm flattered you'd think of me that way, but—"

"I know. It's not my place to try to manipulate who my son marries."

"No." Camille paused. "But if it's any consolation, there's no one in the world I'd rather have for my husband's mother than you. But I really doubt that Nathan and I would get along that well."

"Why do you say that?"

"My mom says my expectations are too high."

"Nathan's like that too."

On her way back to her apartment, Camille debated whether she should have admitted that she had recently dreamed about Nathan. But she dismissed it from her mind as just resulting from her having spent so much time looking at his scrapbook.

▼ ▼ ▼

*Washington, D.C.: Thursday, June 30*

The deadline for placing a want ad in the *Denver Post* for the Sunday edition was Tuesday, but when he began to deal with the paper, Gibbs had sent an additional five hundred dollars cash to the classifieds department manager and asked to be allowed to get his ad in as late as Thursday.

That Thursday Gibbs was in the Washington, D.C. area, in a hotel just outside the capital. He had a meeting set up with Senator Montgomery for Friday afternoon, at which time he would turn over everything he had gathered in his investigation of the illegal activities of Donovan and Steiger. By tomorrow afternoon at five, it would be all over and he could return to a more normal lifestyle.

Gibbs picked up the phone and called the *Denver Post.* He dictated his ad about the puppies, giving the key phrase, "one puppy left," which would bring Nathan Williams out of hiding and home to his family.

▼ ▼ ▼

*Washington, D.C.: Friday, July 1, 7:30 P.M.*

Steiger took one last look at the body of Gibbs sprawled on the floor of the hotel room, then looked around again to make sure nothing would give the police any clues.

Too bad, he thought, that Gibbs had let his guard down after turning over the disk to Senator Montgomery. It was a tragic mistake but understandable. Who would have thought that a respected U.S. senator, a man who had initiated the investigation of drug payoffs to law enforcement personnel, would himself be on the drug dealer's payroll? Steiger smiled as he thought about how easy it had been to get Gibbs. He hadn't had anything against Gibbs personally. He tried not to hate anyone. He just liked to do a good job. Now, with Gibbs out of the way, his next job was to find Williams and the other disk and the girl he was staying with—in that order. They all needed to be destroyed. After that, he'd finish up by disposing of the women in Gibbs's life—his first wife, his daughter, and Rita his second wife. Steiger liked things to be neat and tidy.

But first, Williams and the girl. Maybe he wouldn't have to look too hard. Perhaps they, like Gibbs, would come to Montgomery too.

All roads led to Montgomery, and from Montgomery they led to him.

But, as Donovan had said once, they were not roads.

They were dead ends.

▼ ▼ ▼

*Minneapolis, Minnesota: Saturday afternoon, July 2*

Steiger took the afternoon flight from Washington, D.C., to Minneapolis. His flight to Rapid City was scheduled to leave two hours later, but fifteen minutes before they were to board, there was an announcement that the flight had been cancelled due to mechanical problems.

Steiger went to the desk. "Excuse me. Can you tell me when your next flight to Rapid City is?" he asked the pretty female agent.

"Tomorrow morning at seven-thirty."

"Gosh, that is really disappointing. You see, I have some important business I need to attend to tomorrow."

"I'm sorry, sir," she said.

"That's all right. It's not your fault. I know you're doing the best you can."

"Thank you. So many people get mad at us. It's like they think we go out and mess with the plane during our break just so people will miss their flight."

He touched her hand lightly. "I try never to get mad. A bad temper can be a terrible thing."

She liked this man. "That is so true. You know, it's people like you that make this a better world."

He smiled. "Thank you. I try to do my part."

He went off to see about getting a chartered flight that night to Rapid City. But half an hour later a heavy storm stalled over Minneapolis, and all air travel shut down. It was useless. He was stuck in Minneapolis until morning.

▼ ▼ ▼

*Pine Ridge, South Dakota: Saturday, July 2*

Wearing white slacks and a white shirt, Nathan watched as Jessica, also dressed in white, came out of the dressing room at the Pine Ridge meetinghouse. She looked like royalty, even in a plain white dress. She smiled and reached out for his hand and together they walked to the first row of the chapel.

Twenty or so people had gathered in the small meetinghouse—the missionary couple who had taught Jessica, two young missionary elders, and several Lakota members who had heard about her baptism.

Nathan had been thrilled when Jessica had asked him to baptize her. It seemed a fitting, though unexpected, conclusion to his missionary service.

The baptismal service was short and to the point: an opening song, a prayer, and a brief talk about baptism by one of the elders. And then they went to the font. Nathan went down the stairs into the warm water first. He extended his hand to Jessica as she came down the steps, and they moved to the center of the font. And then the upraised hand, the sacred prayer, and the rapid immersion in the water. After she came up out of the water and the two elders acting as witnesses had nodded their approval, Jessica unexpectedly lifted both hands in the air and said, *"Mitakuyepi."*

One of the older Lakota women smiled, nodded her approval, and softly repeated the word Jessica had used. Jessica turned to the woman and smiled, then walked up the stairs to change.

A few minutes later the small group gathered once again. Jessica wore the traditional dress she danced in at powwows, and on her feet she wore beaded moccasins.

"What did you say after you were baptized?" Nathan whispered.

*"Mitakuyepi.* It means 'all my relatives.' It's like you calling members of the Church brothers and sisters."

The meeting continued with a talk about the gift of the Holy Ghost, and then, at her request, Nathan confirmed Jessica a member of the Church. He felt prompted to promise her that she would bless the lives of many of her people and that through her faithfulness in the Church she would be able to do more good than she could ever have done otherwise. He could not stop himself from giving the blessing he gave, and a part of him felt some sadness;

he sensed that the blessing he gave her would somehow take her away from him.

When he finished, she stood up and they embraced.

After the meeting, members of the branch enthusiastically welcomed Jessica. The branch had not experienced much growth for years, and Nathan could see the members were excited to have someone like Jessica, young and strong in her convictions, accept the gospel and become a part of them.

Nathan enjoyed watching as Jessica spoke Lakota with the branch members. He had always been taught that Indians were a stoic people who never laughed, but, like many things he'd been taught, that was not true either. Although he couldn't understand the words, he could understand the love their words conveyed.

Brother and Sister Cummings, the missionary couple who had taught Jessica, appeared to have also adopted her. They clearly adored her. Brother Cummings used up nearly a roll of film having Nathan take pictures of him and his wife standing proudly with Jessica.

▼ ▼ ▼

At nine-thirty that night Nathan and Jessica finally left Pine Ridge for Rapid City. They arrived at eleven-fifteen, and she suggested that they go to Sheridan Lake to wait until the *Denver Post* was delivered.

They paid for a campsite and found one far away from other campers. Then they gathered some wood, made a fire, and sat by it and talked. Things were different now between them. At first Nathan wasn't sure what it was, but then he realized they were treating each other as if they were brother and sister. It was more than just the fact that she had been baptized. It was something else.

"I have something to give you," she said.

"What for?"

"To honor you for leading me to the truth."

"I don't have anything for you."

She shook her head. "Don't ever say that when someone wishes to honor you." She held up a white shirt with strips of red, yellow, white, and black ribbon sewn onto it and said, "This is called a ribbon shirt. It's worn at powwows. After you've been home, I hope you'll come back and let us honor you at a pow-wow." She gently placed the shirt on his lap.

"Thank you very much."

As the night drew on, the need for speaking diminished, and they sat huddled next to each other, watching the dying embers of the fire.

At four-thirty they headed back to Rapid City. Nathan didn't even dare to hope that he'd be home by the end of the day. He would just take whatever came. Besides, had it not been for the extra week he had had to stay in South Dakota, Jessica might never have been baptized.

By the time he pulled into the parking lot of the convenience store, the Sunday issue of the *Denver Post* had already been placed in the rack outside. Nathan put his quarters in the machine, then took the newspaper back to the Jimmy and got in. He gave the paper to Jessica and asked her to look for the want ad and tell him what it said.

"Here it is," she said.

"What does it say?"

"'One puppy left.'"

"Are you serious?"

"'One puppy left.' Here it is, read it for yourself."

"One puppy left," he read. Suddenly the realization hit him. He was going home! They jumped out of the Jimmy, ran around behind the vehicle, threw their arms around each other, and began dancing in the empty parking lot, chanting, "One puppy left!"

Then they went inside the store. "Good morning!" Nathan practically shouted at the woman at the counter. "Isn't this a beautiful morning?"

"If you say so."

"We want some milk and two of the gooiest cinnamon buns you've got. We're here to celebrate!"

"What's the occasion?"

"My friend had some puppies for sale, and now he's only got one left. Isn't that great? That means I get to go home."

"Let me guess—you folks are from Denver, right?"

▼ ▼ ▼

Nathan and Jessica were among the first to enter the Rapid City airport terminal that morning. Before he called his parents, Nathan made sure he had the ticket to Salt Lake City and on to Idaho Falls. He didn't want to call and then find out the plane was full. He had no trouble buying a ticket. He paid cash.

At a few minutes to eight he stood before a pay phone, with Jessica at his side, and dialed his home phone.

▼ ▼ ▼

*Rexburg, Idaho: Sunday, July 3, 7:57 A.M.*

Boyd was shaving when he heard the phone ring in the hallway. He rushed out to answer it so it wouldn't wake Elaine up. She couldn't sleep at night because of worrying about Nathan and often stayed up until two or three in the morning before finally dropping off to sleep.

"Hello," he said, picking up the cordless phone.

"Dad! Hello, it's me, Nathan. Hope I didn't wake you up!"

"Nathan? Is that really you? Where are you? Are you okay?"

"I'm fine now, Dad. There were some men who wanted to kill me, so I had to hide out for a while. But it's okay for me to come home now."

"When will you be home?"

"I'll be there today."

"That's great! Let me put your mother on the phone." Boyd hurried into the bedroom. "It's Nathan!" he called out, handing her the phone. And then he ran to Kim's room. "Nathan's on the phone! He's coming home today!"

"Oh, Nathan! I can't believe it," his mother exclaimed through her tears. "Where are you?"

"I'm in Rapid City, South Dakota. I'll tell you all about it. I'm sorry I've put you through so much, but there was nothing else I could do. I was told that if I let you know what was happening, you and Dad would be in danger too. But it's all over now, and I'm coming home. I made reservations to fly into Idaho Falls so you won't have to drive so far to get me. I'll be getting in at one o'clock this afternoon."

"You're coming home. I'm so grateful you're all right. We've all been sick with worry."

Nathan talked to his father again and then to Kim. Never one for ambiguities, Kim asked, "Have you been living with a girl while you were away?"

"No, why?"

"I don't know. That's what some people are saying."

"I haven't done anything wrong."

"That's what I told 'em."

▼ ▼ ▼

*Rapid City Regional Airport: Sunday, July 3, 8:22 A.M.*

The flight from Rapid City to Salt Lake City was scheduled to leave at nine o'clock that morning. Jessica asked Nathan to put on the ribbon shirt she'd given him because she wanted to find someone to take a picture of them both before he left. She went to the women's rest room to change into her traditional buckskin dress.

He finished changing first and stepped out into the terminal to wait for her. A flight from Minneapolis had just landed, and passengers were beginning to stream into the waiting area and past the place where Nathan was standing.

Looking at the crowd Nathan was shocked to see Steiger coming toward him. He caught his breath and his heart began to race. He wanted to run, but he knew that would give him away. *He found out where I was hiding,* he thought, *and he's come here to kill both Jessica and me.*

Steiger was coming closer; he would pass within five feet of Nathan.

Nathan glanced at his reflection in a display case. It was true what Jessica had said—he could pass for Indian. It was his only chance. He turned partially away so Steiger couldn't get a good look at his face.

Steiger paid no attention to him and continued on with the rest of the passengers down the hall to the airport's main entrance. Once he was out of sight, Nathan stuck his head into the entrance of the women's rest room. "Jessica," he called out. "Hurry up!"

When she came out, he said, "We're in trouble. I just saw Steiger get off a plane. He must know about you and me. Can you call somebody to go get your grandmother and take her away from her house for a few days?"

"I'll call my aunt."

He touched her arm. "I'm sorry you ever got involved in this."

"It'll be okay."

Nathan went down the escalator to the baggage area just as Steiger was leaving a rental-car counter. Nathan waited until he saw Steiger drive away from the parking lot, then went back upstairs to find Jessica.

"He's gone," Nathan said. "Did you reach your aunt?"

"Yes. She's on her way to pick up my grandmother."

"Let's get out of here." They started walking for the exit.

"Where are we going?" she asked.

"It doesn't matter where we go so long as Steiger can't find us. Have you ever been to Glacier National Park in Montana?"

"No."

"I was there with my parents once on a vacation. If we went backpacking in the wilderness areas, it'd be nearly impossible for anyone to find us."

"For how long?"

"I don't know."

"Glacier Park sounds okay to me," she said.

As much as Nathan wanted to call his parents and tell them he wasn't coming, he knew that to do so might give them away. He did not want to give Steiger any information.

They headed west on I-90 on their way to Glacier Park. While Nathan drove, Jessica read the rest of the Sunday *Denver Post* they'd bought earlier that morning. Suddenly she cried out, "Oh no!"

"What's the matter?" he asked.

"Pull over and stop. Hurry up!"

He slowed down and stopped. "What's wrong?"

"Gibbs is dead. He was murdered. I just read it in the paper."

Nathan felt stunned. She handed him the paper and he read an article entitled "FBI Agent's Murder Remains Mystery." It said that Gibbs had been shot in a motel room near Washington, D.C., and that there were no clues.

"I can't believe it," Nathan said. "If they got to Gibbs, then what chance do we have?"

"We have as good a chance as anyone."

"Whoever killed him must have gotten to him before he was able to meet with Senator Montgomery."

"We're the only ones now who can get the information to Montgomery," Jessica said.

There was only one choice for them—to go to Washington, D.C., and give the disk to Senator Montgomery.

*Idaho Falls, Idaho: Sunday, July 3, 10:32 A.M.*

On the way to Idaho Falls, Elaine gave Kim a blue Magic Marker and some butcher paper and had her write "Welcome home, Nathan!" so they'd have something in the way of a banner to hold up at the airport.

Because the Salt Lake City flight was on a small plane, it didn't take long for Nathan's parents to realize he was not one of the passengers.

"Why isn't he here?" Kim asked.

"Something must have happened."

"Something is always happening."

"Do you want to wait for the next flight?" Boyd asked.

Elaine felt numb. "No, let's just go home."

*On the road to Washington, D.C.: July 3–5*

Nathan and Jessica worked out a system that would allow them to get across the country in the least possible time. He would drive three hours while she slept in the backseat, and then she would drive and Nathan would sleep. They stopped only for gasoline, food, and to use the rest room.

Once at a deserted rest stop, while he waited for Jessica, Nathan set a soda pop can on a hill and tried to shoot it with Steiger's gun. Out of three tries, he hit it once. He was not at all confident that he would come out on top if he had to shoot his way out of a confrontation with Steiger. Even so, it was all they had.

At first they didn't talk much. They were both tired from staying up the night before, and the one who wasn't driving was usually sleeping.

They stayed on Interstate 90 to Albert Lea, Minnesota, and then turned south on Interstate 35. By eleven o'clock that night they both were too tired to drive, so they pulled into a rest stop to sleep.

*Monday, July 4*

They slept until seven-thirty in the morning and then took off again. They might not have even known it was the Fourth of July except for references to it on the radio.

"What if Senator Montgomery isn't in Washington?" Jessica asked. "For all we know, maybe he's spending the Fourth of July on the West Coast. I think we should at least call him."

Nathan decided what she said made sense. The next town they came to, they tried to get his phone number from directory assistance. It took them fifteen minutes because Montgomery lived in a suburb community in Virginia, but eventually they got his number.

In Virginia it was ten-fifteen when they placed the call. Senator Montgomery's wife answered the phone.

"May I speak to Senator Montgomery?" Nathan asked. "It's very important."

"He's in the shower now. Can you call back?"

"No, please, this is very important. Go talk to him."

"Who shall I say is calling?"

"Is there any chance someone else might be listening to us?"

"No, we have a protected line," she said.

"Tell your husband I worked for Gibbs."

"All right, just a minute."

When Montgomery came on the phone, the reception was good enough for Nathan to hear the shower being turned off. "Hello. Who is this?" the senator barked. He sounded annoyed.

"Senator Montgomery, you don't know me, but I have some information that Agent Gibbs of the FBI gave to me on June 9," Nathan responded.

"What kind of information?"

"It's a computer disk. Gibbs told me if I didn't hear from him, I should contact you. He said you'd know what to do with it."

"Do you know that Gibbs was murdered last week?" Montgomery asked.

Nathan said weakly, "Yes, I know. We saw the report in the paper."

"I was, of course, shocked at the news. He never even got a chance to talk to me. That means the information on your disk is even more important. It is vital that I get that disk as soon as possible. Don't trust anyone else with it except me. Do you understand?"

"Yes, of course."

"Where are you now?"

He looked outside the phone booth. "I'm not exactly sure, but I'm pretty sure we can get to you by tomorrow morning."

"All right, but hurry up. And if you have any trouble, let me know and I'll send someone to meet you."

"We'll be fine. Where do you want us to come?"

"To my office in the Senate Office Building on Capitol Hill. How about tomorrow afternoon at two? Take it easy and don't have any accidents. We need that disk."

▼ ▼ ▼

Two minutes later Montgomery contacted Steiger on the Pine Ridge Reservation by cellular phone. "Get back here as soon as you can," he said. "Our boy is coming to see me tomorrow afternoon in my office."

"I'm on my way."

▼ ▼ ▼

Nathan stopped around midnight at a rest stop near Williamsport, Maryland. Jessica woke up when they stopped moving, sat up, and looked around. "Where are we?"

"About an hour from Washington. Let's sleep until morning."

# CHAPTER ELEVEN

*Tuesday, July 5*

NATHAN AWOKE TO THE SOUND OF SONGBIRDS. He looked at his watch. It was eight-thirty in the morning. He wondered if this was the last day of his life and if he would ever again hear the morning song of birds. He had lived all his life around them and yet had ignored their song.

He used the rest room, washed up, then returned to the Jimmy. He reached back where Jessica was curled up on the backseat and touched her shoulder. She opened her eyes. "It's morning," he said.

"What time is it?"

"Quarter to nine."

She spotted the rest rooms nearby and said, "I'll be back in a minute."

When she came out of the rest room a few minutes later, she walked past a trucker on his way to the rest room after a long night of driving. As she passed, he turned and stared at her.

When she got back in the Jimmy, Nathan told her what had happened. "That guy you just walked by drove all night, but he's awake now," he teased.

"Stop," she said with a smile.

Because he wasn't sure if they'd make it through the day alive, it seemed like a time to say what was in his heart. He reached for her hand. "You know I love you, don't you?"

"Yes, I know that. I love you too, Nathan."

"I wanted you to know—just in case."

"Thank you. You're my best friend and my teacher."

"You don't have to go on to Washington with me. You could stay here. We could get you a place to stay and you could wait for me."

"No, I'm going with you."

"It might be dangerous."

"If it is, you'll need me to help you."

"I don't want you to get hurt."

She shrugged. "This is a good day to die."

It caught him by surprise. "Why did you say that?"

"It's what Lakota warriors used to say before going into battle."

"If we get out of this alive, I think we should talk about getting married," he said.

"It would be wonderful to be married to you, Nathan. I really mean that."

"Good. It's settled then."

"First let's see if we can get through today," she said.

"Are you worried?" he asked.

"I just don't know what to expect, that's all. What about you?"

"Someone killed Gibbs and he was a professional. Yeah, I'm worried."

"Could we read together like we used to and then have prayer? That might help."

They sat together in the backseat. Nathan picked up his rain-soaked, battered, and bent copy of the Book of Mormon and read: "Cry unto him for mercy; for he is mighty to save. Yea, humble yourselves, and continue in prayer unto him. Cry unto him when ye are in your fields, yea, over all your flocks. Cry unto him in your houses, yea, over all your household, both morning, midday, and evening. Yea, cry unto him against the power of your enemies." He stopped reading. "Steiger scares me," he said softly. "I've had nightmares about him."

Jessica wanted to pray outside. She took his hand and led him into a clump of trees, where they knelt on the ground and each said a prayer. They could hear the sound of traffic on the interstate, but there, among the trees, it was quiet and peaceful.

When they were finished praying, they stood up and held each other, and then it was time to go.

They had no desire to face rush-hour traffic, so they drove to a nearby restaurant for breakfast. Neither of them was hungry, but they knew they needed to eat.

"You told me about Gibbs's wife," Jessica said. "Maybe we should call her and find out what she knows."

"I don't even know where they lived."

"It was in the Seattle area though, right?"

"I think so."

"Let me see what I can do."

"I'll be in the Jimmy," he said.

While she used a pay phone outside the restaurant, he sat in the driver's seat and practiced putting ammunition into the gun. He was slow and clumsy and kept dropping bullets. It seemed so useless. What chance would he have in a gunfight with Steiger?

Half an hour later she came running out to the Jimmy. "I found Mrs. Gibbs! She's on the line. She wants to talk to you. Hurry!"

"Is this a protected line?" he asked Mrs. Gibbs when he picked up the phone.

"I don't know. Dave was the expert on things like that. To tell you the truth, I'm scared. I've been on the run since I got home from the funeral. Right now I'm talking to you on a cellular phone out on the highway. I was hoping you'd call. Do you still have the disk Dave gave you?"

"Yes. We've got it."

"Be careful, okay?"

"We will. What can you tell me about how your husband was killed?"

"He was shot. They found him in a motel room about half an hour from Senator Montgomery's office. I talked to Montgomery, and he said Dave never contacted him. So whoever killed him has the disk." She paused. "There's something about this that doesn't make sense though."

"What?"

"When Dave opened the door and let his killer in, he wasn't even holding his gun. The police found it in a drawer in the dresser. Dave was never that careless to let his guard down like that. It just doesn't make sense."

▼ ▼ ▼

*Senate Office Building, Washington, D.C.: Tuesday, July 5*

From the time they left the Jimmy in the parking lot and started walking toward the Senate Office Building, they kept looking around for any sign of Steiger. Nathan feared a sniper's bullet because that was an enemy you couldn't even face before it cut you down. He had left Steiger's gun behind in the Jimmy. He didn't feel confident it would do him any good.

At two o'clock that afternoon Nathan and Jessica entered Senator Michael Montgomery's office. His staff members were all away. The senator had worked them until one-thirty and then sent them off for a late lunch.

Senator Montgomery was waiting for them, a warm, cordial smile on his face. After shaking their hands, he came right to the point. "Do you have the disk?" he asked.

"Yes. Here it is."

Montgomery took it and put it in the center drawer of his desk. "You two have the thanks of an entire nation for what you've done. This will help bring drug trafficking to a stop in the Northwest. As soon as everyone connected with this is arrested, I'm going to recommend to the president that you both be given medals of valor."

Nathan put his arm around Jessica and pulled her toward him. "Thank you, sir. It's been hard at times, but right now it all feels worthwhile."

"I'm sure you're anxious to contact your families and let them know you're okay and then head home. But the FBI would like you to hole-up here for another twenty-four hours. By then they'll have arrested everyone connected with this operation. If you phone home or start making airline reservations, I'm afraid that will tip Donovan off. Are you willing to lay low for another day?"

"Well, sure, I guess so," Nathan said.

"While you're here, please, let my wife and me take you out to dinner tonight," the senator said. "I have taken the liberty of reserving the executive suite for you at one of the nicest hotels in town. We'll pick you up for dinner, and then you can rest up tonight before you head back home."

"Oh, that's very kind, but we . . . " Nathan was about to say they'd need two rooms, not one.

Jessica interrupted him. "That sounds great. I'd love to spend one more night with Nathan before we go our separate ways."

Nathan's mouth dropped open, but he didn't say anything because he trusted Jessica. Senator Montgomery handed him the key to the hotel room, gave him directions on how to get there, and said that he and his wife would pick them up at six-thirty that evening.

On the way to the parking lot, Jessica looked at him strangely. "Don't you have something to say?"

"Yes. Why only one room?"

She gave him a seductive smile. "Because one room is what we'll need for what I have in mind."

"We can't let our guard down now," he said.

"I know. That's where Gibbs went wrong, isn't it?" Jessica said.

"What are you talking about?" he asked.

"I kept thinking about what Mrs. Gibbs said—that it wasn't like her husband to have been so careless. Then it occurred to me—what if Gibbs was killed after he gave the disk to Montgomery?" Without waiting for his reaction, she added, "We're going to have a night we'll never forget."

▼ ▼ ▼

Steiger and Montgomery walked quickly down the hall from the elevator to the executive suite of the hotel. Steiger stood to one side while the senator knocked on the door.

"Who is it?" Nathan asked.

"It's Michael Montgomery. My wife and I are here to take you to dinner."

From behind the door Nathan called out, "Just a minute. We're running a little behind schedule. I guess we . . . uh . . . kind of fell asleep. Jessica is still sleeping."

"That's okay. You and I can go down for a drink while we wait for her to get ready."

As the door opened, Montgomery stepped aside, and Steiger slipped into the darkened hotel room. The only light came from a fluorescent glow through the partially open bathroom door. He stepped quickly to the side of the bed and pumped two quick shots into the figure of a woman that lay under the covers. The silencer on his gun muffled the reports so that nobody outside the room could have heard anything.

Then, continuing to point his gun at the figure in the bed, he reached out cautiously and snatched the blanket away, only to discover an arrangement of pillows and the head of a dark-haired female mannequin.

Just at that moment two FBI agents lunged from a closet behind Steiger, and the next thing he knew, he was disarmed and lying face down on the bed with his hands cuffed behind him.

Meanwhile, Senator Montgomery, sensing that something had gone wrong, hurried to his car, where he was intercepted and also arrested by federal agents.

Nathan and Jessica had never been in any danger. Once Nathan had answered Senator Montgomery through the door, he had been ushered to an adjoining room in the suite. Only after everything was safe did the police let Nathan and Jessica leave the hotel.

They emerged from the lobby of the hotel just in time to see Montgomery and Steiger being driven away by the police. Minutes later, in Montgomery's senate office, the FBI recovered both disks. The information on the disks was enough to expose the full extent of Donovan's operation.

Just as Jessica had promised, it had been a night Nathan would never forget.

# CHAPTER TWELVE

*Tuesday night, July 5*

DONOVAN AND SEVERAL OTHERS WERE ARRESTED late that night in Seattle.

Nathan and Jessica spent the night at the home of an FBI agent, a member of the Church, who had been in on the arrest of Steiger and Montgomery. He was married and had three children. He let Nathan use his phone to contact his parents and explain everything. It was an hour-long conversation. And then Kim came on the line.

"When are you coming home?" she asked.

"I don't know. Maybe tomorrow."

"Do me a favor, okay? Get to the airport before you call. I'm really getting tired of waiting around for you."

*Wednesday, July 6*

Nathan and Jessica spent Wednesday morning giving a detailed statement to the police and FBI. It was only then they learned that the behind-the-scenes inquiries about Donovan made by James Doyle of Church Security had made it so Nathan and Jessica were listened to when they went to the FBI for help.

At noon they were part of a press conference. They spent the next hour being interviewed by TV reporters.

Finally they escaped. Jessica dropped Nathan off at Dulles

International Airport around six o'clock that night. Her plan was to drive to South Dakota in what was now her GMC Jimmy.

Nathan did not phone his parents until his flight landed in Salt Lake City. His flight from Salt Lake City to Idaho Falls arrived at ten-thirty that night. As he stepped into the terminal of the Idaho Falls airport, he saw his parents and Kim holding a sign they had hastily scribbled on the back of a box they found in a wastepaper basket just minutes before Nathan's plane had landed.

Nathan threw his arms around his mother. "Oh, Mom." It was all he could say.

"You're home, you're finally home." Tears were streaming down her face.

"I'm sorry for making you worry, Mom."

"You're safe. That's all that counts." She looked tired but happy.

"Welcome home, son," his father said, pulling Nathan in close and holding him tight.

"It's good to be home again." And it was true. For the first time since June ninth, he felt safe.

So they wouldn't just stand around and bawl, Nathan said to his dad, "Probably the reason you missed me is because you were worried I wouldn't be around for spud harvest this year, right?"

His father broke into a grin. "Not really. You do so little work when you're here, I'm not sure we'd have even known the difference."

"Well if that's the case, maybe I'll take a vacation next spud harvest."

"No need to do that. I could probably find something for you to do."

Nathan turned to face Kim. "Oh, my gosh! Would you look at this? Who is this beautiful woman standing here? I've got to meet this girl . . . wait a minute . . . hold on . . . is this my sister? I can't believe it! I can see I'm going to have to get a big stick to beat away all the boys who are going to start coming to the door."

"You're too late," his mother said. "They're already circling the house."

"Oh, Mom," Kim said with an embarrassed but proud smile.

Nathan gathered Kim into his arms. "I'm so glad you're my sister."

She put her head on his shoulder. "I prayed for you every night," she said.

"Believe me—your prayers made a big difference."

"Do you have any luggage?" his father asked.

"Just the stuff in this backpack," he said.

"Do you remember that old TV you let me use when you left?" Kim asked. "Well, it doesn't work anymore."

Nathan wrapped his arm around her neck. "I'm sure we can work something out . . . " He squeezed lightly and then said in a threatening voice, " . . . like, maybe you can make my bed for a year."

"A year? That's way too long."

"How long then?"

"Maybe a week."

He shrugged his shoulders. "It doesn't matter. I don't care about that old TV. I don't care about anything. I'm just glad to be home."

Kim saw her chance. "In that case—remember the leather jacket you left in your closet when you left on your mission?"

▼ ▼ ▼

For the next few days Nathan and Jessica were in the news as the details of how they helped to expose a major illicit drug operation became known. Nathan thought about turning down all offers to be interviewed, but his father suggested it might be good publicity for the Church. So for the next week he did little else except talk in front of TV cameras. He always made sure to mention the sacrifice Dave Gibbs of the FBI had made to bring Donovan and Steiger to justice. He also tried to work into the interview that he had been serving a mission and that he felt the only reason he and Jessica had been able to do what they did was because God answered their prayers.

For her part, Jessica decided to use her brief and fleeting moment of fame to talk about Indian issues. In her interview on *Oprah,* she took strong exception to the demeaning use of Native American symbols by teams such as the Atlanta Braves,

Cleveland Indians, and Washington Redskins. In her interview on *Nightline,* she promoted higher education for Indians, emphasizing that the warriors of today are those who get a good education.

▼ ▼ ▼

*Seattle, Washington: August*

Todd Donovan waited for his father to be brought to the visitor area. This was the first time he had come to see him. When the news stories about his father's crimes had first surfaced, reporters had camped outside the Donovans' house waiting for anyone who might try to leave. Todd had gone to Europe to escape. His father's trial was scheduled for October, but Todd was told that the defense lawyers would probably try to get it postponed until spring.

Todd would be a sophomore at Harvard fall semester, or at least he would be if he could come up with enough money to pay his tuition. Up to now his father had paid for his schooling, but that seemed to have come to an end.

Wearing an orange jumpsuit, Jack Donovan was admitted to the visitors cell. He was separated from Todd by a thick glass partition, so they spoke through microphones. Jack looked ten years older than he had the last time Todd had seen him.

Todd wanted to confine their meeting to light conversation. He didn't want to admit how embarrassed he was that his father was a criminal. He didn't want to reveal that his mother was talking to a lawyer about filing for a divorce.

His father rambled on about his bad fortune in being caught. He blamed Nathan Williams and Jessica Red Willow for everything. "They should be made to pay for what they've done to our family."

"What are you talking about?" Todd asked.

"You're the only one I can count on now. They need to be punished." His father leaned forward and slowly and silently mouthed the words: "I want you to kill them."

"Are you crazy? I'm not doing anything like that."

"Do you have a piece of paper?"

Todd pulled out his wallet and found a card he could write on. He found a pen in his sportcoat pocket. Jack mouthed six numbers. Todd wrote them down. He realized the precautions were necessary because their conversation was being monitored.

Todd looked at the number. "What is this?"

"Do you remember where we used to go for summer vacations?"

When Todd was a boy, before they moved to Seattle, the Donovans had lived in Boston, and every summer they would spend a month near Lake Winnesquam in New Hampshire. "Yeah, sure."

"Do you remember me taking you to get an ice-cream cone every Friday? That brings back good memories for me. What about you?"

Todd remembered the trips. Once a week his father would take Todd with him to a bank, where he seemed to be good friends with a Mr. Sullivan, the bank president. They always spent a few minutes in Mr. Sullivan's office, where someone would bring a sealed envelope. Afterwards Jack always bought Todd an ice-cream cone. He wondered if the number his father had given him might be for a savings account in the bank.

"You have three years of school left," his dad said. "If you accept my help, it's with the understanding that you need to do something for me. If you do what I want you to do, there will be more, much more, for you. Just think about it."

The next day Todd went to the public library, where he looked through some New Hampshire phone books. He couldn't remember the name of the bank where Mr. Sullivan worked, so he copied down the phone numbers of several banks in the Lake Winnesquam area. That afternoon he began calling some of the banks, asking for the balance in an account with the number his father had given him.

On his fourth call, after he had given the number to a teller, he was put on hold, and then Mr. Sullivan came on the line. "Who is calling, please?"

"Todd Donovan. My dad used to bring me with him to your bank when we stayed at the lake during the summer."

Mr. Sullivan asked several questions that only Todd would know the answers to. Then, satisfied it was Todd, he told him there was $150,000 in a savings account his father had set up for him several years ago.

"What do I need to do to withdraw some of the money?" Todd asked.

"Just come and see me."

"I don't need any now. I just wanted to know that it's there."

Todd knew that if he used the money, his father would think he had agreed to kill Nathan Williams and Jessica Red Willow. But he was not a killer, so to avoid having to use the money, he got a job working on campus.

Two weeks into the semester, though, he met a girl named Bridget. Bridget came from a rich family, and she didn't understand why Todd had to work all the time or why he wasn't driving a newer car.

A month later he quit his job so he could spend more time with her. In order to meet expenses, he withdrew a few thousand dollars from the account his father had set up for him, promising himself to pay it back next summer.

▼ ▼ ▼

*July–September*

What really helped Nathan adjust to being home was working with his dad on the farm. In August they harvested grain and began preparing for the spud harvest which would begin in October. The potato harvest was a regional holiday. School was even let out to give students a chance to earn some money.

That fall Jessica was a junior at the South Dakota School of Mines and Technology in Rapid City, where she spent much of her time helping students in the Native American Study Center. She also went to church every Sunday and attended an institute class on the Book of Mormon once a week. She was called to be a visiting teacher and assigned to visit some of the Indian members of the church who lived in Lakota Homes.

▼ ▼ ▼

*Rexburg, Idaho: September*

"There's a girl I'd like you to meet sometime," Elaine said a couple of weeks after fall semester began at Ricks College. "She's taking voice lessons from me again this year. Her name is Camille Stoddard. Because her brother is on a mission, her family doesn't have a lot of extra money, so she helps me do housework. Oh, one other thing, she was raised on a farm."

Nathan looked at his mother skeptically.

"She looks like that girl on *Northern Exposure,*" his mother said.

"I'm really only interested in Jessica."

"I know, but it wouldn't hurt to at least meet Camille."

"It might not hurt, but it probably wouldn't do much good either."

Elaine decided to wait a little longer.

Because she didn't want Nathan thinking of Camille as the hired help, Elaine arranged for her to work when Nathan wasn't home.

One day near the end of September, however, Nathan came home unexpectedly. Elaine had just left to go to the store when he walked into the house. The bathroom door was closed, but he could hear the water being turned on and off. There was also a woman in the bathroom, singing at the top of her voice. He dropped his books off in his room and went to the kitchen for milk and cookies.

A few minutes later the bathroom door opened, and a young woman came out. He realized she was probably the person his mother had talked to him about. He vaguely remembered that her name was Camille.

As she walked into the kitchen carrying the mop and bucket she had been using, she was still singing enthusiastically. Then she saw Nathan sitting at the kitchen table. "Oh my gosh! I didn't know anyone was here. I'm really sorry."

"Don't be. It was good. I enjoyed listening to you."

"You must be Nathan."

"Right. And you're Camille?"

"Yes."

Her hair was dark brown and short. She wore no lipstick but made up for it by what she had done with her eyes. He was sure that any other guy would have been impressed. His main complaint was that she wasn't Jessica.

"How long have you been here?" she asked.

"Not long."

"You should have said something."

"I didn't want you to stop because it sounded like you were having such a good time."

"I was." She looked at him more carefully. "You're nicer than I thought you'd be."

"What did you think I'd be like?"

"The Terminator," she said, trying to imitate Arnold Schwarzenegger. When she smiled, she showed more teeth than any girl he'd ever known. He suspected it was because she was a singer. Her mother had once tried to show him some exercises that involved lifting the upper lip in singing various vowels. He had, of course, ignored the advice. Apparently Camille had not.

"You want some milk and cookies?" he asked.

"Sure, why not?"

As they talked about school, he couldn't help comparing her to Jessica. When Jessica spoke, it was soft and mellow, like a gentle breeze through a stand of cottonwood trees. When Camille spoke, it was with precision. She enunciated each diphthong and syllable, but there was a musical quality to her voice. His mother spoke the same way.

A few minutes later they heard his mother pull into the driveway. "Well, I'd better get back to work," Camille said. "Your mother isn't paying me to sit around and talk to you."

Nathan smiled. "No, but I think she would. She speaks very highly of you."

"Thanks. That picture you have in your bedroom—is that Jessica?"

"You've been in my bedroom?"

"Yes, when I vacuum."

"Oh, yeah, sure. Yes, that's Jessica."

"She's very beautiful. Are you two engaged?"

"Not yet, but I want to marry her someday," Nathan said.

They heard the car door slam as his mother started inside.

Camille nodded. "I can see why. Thanks for the cookies."

▼ ▼ ▼

*October–November*

"Hello," Jessica said as she answered the phone at eleven-thirty on a Tuesday night in October.

"Where have you been?" Nathan asked.

"It was my night to be a tutor for our freshmen at the study center."

"Do you ever get a chance to study for your own classes?"

"Sure. I'm doing okay. But I love working at the study center. I'm sure getting good at trigonometry and algebra. That's what a lot of our freshmen are taking."

"I've been trying to get you for two hours."

"Sorry, but I've been real busy. Tomorrow we're going to visit some schools on the reservation."

"What for?"

"To let 'em know it doesn't take a genius to get a college education. They asked me for sure to go along." She paused. "That was a joke, Nathan."

Nathan was in no mood for jokes. "I miss you so much," he said.

"I miss you too."

"How about if I come to see you next weekend?" he said.

"Next weekend? Let's see . . . that might not be very good."

"Why not?"

"It's the All-Indian basketball tournament at the civic center. We're going to have a booth there. They asked me to be in charge of it. I'll be busy most of the weekend. Sorry."

"What about the weekend after that?"

"That's the national AISES conference." She pronounced it like *ace-sis.*

"What's AISES?"

"American Indian Science and Engineering Society. The conference this year is in Spokane, Washington. Why don't you go?"

"I'm not Indian."

"It doesn't matter. There will be lots of people there who aren't. I'm serious. I know you'd love it, and it would give us a chance to spend some time together. Spokane's not that far from where you live, is it?"

▼ ▼ ▼

Nathan did attend the AISES conference the first weekend in November. For both him and Jessica, the convention was a safe place where they could be together without generating raised eyebrows or having to deal with reporters. There were three thousand Native American college students at the meeting. Nathan found it amazing that he felt so welcome even though he was not Indian. Before every meal, a prayer was offered. In one of the talks, spirituality was identified as one of the characteristics of the complete man or woman.

At the banquet held at the close of the conference, Jessica was honored for her courage and leadership. A videotape was shown of clips from interviews where she had spoken out in behalf of AISES and Indian issues. She was given a ceremonial blanket.

While accepting her award, she asked Nathan to join her at the microphone. As he was walking to the stage, she said, "This is my friend Nathan Williams. He wishes he were Indian. Someday he'll probably be chief of the Wannabe Tribe," she joked. "Seriously, he has helped me in so many ways. I have the greatest respect and admiration for him. Nathan, is there anything you want to say to my friends?"

Nathan stepped to the microphone and began speaking. "They say that to know a person, you need to walk in his moccasins for a mile. For a few weeks last summer I walked in your moccasins, and that experience has changed my life forever. I will never be the same. The lesson I learned while getting to know something of your culture is that every person, regardless of the color of their skin, is important. I learned that lesson from Jessica first and now, this week, I have learned it from you. *Mitakuyepi!*"

Jessica came forward and slipped the blanket over his shoulders. He thought it was only temporary, but she meant for him to keep it. After the ceremony he tried to talk her out of it, but she wouldn't listen to him.

After the banquet there was a powwow. It was his first pow-wow. Jessica took part in many of the songs and traditional dances while he stood on the sidelines wearing the ribbon shirt she'd given him. When the honor dance began, she came and got him. They stood side by side, and she showed him the step. Then together they danced the honor dance around the hotel ballroom.

Two members of AISES who were attending BYU came up and started talking to Jessica. Before they left, they asked her to speak at BYU's Lamanite Week in the spring.

Nathan and Jessica stayed at the powwow until one in the morning, and then he walked her to her room. People were still milling around, so there was no chance for any privacy in the hall-way. Her door was open when they got there. Her three room-mates were in the room watching a movie.

"It's hard to believe we spent so much time together, just the two of us, and now we can't find five minutes to be by ourselves," Nathan said.

She smiled. "They say you're never alone at an AISES con-vention."

"Is there someplace we can go where we can be alone?"

"I don't think there is."

He tried to hold her in his arms, but she shook her head. "Not here. There are too many people around."

"I feel like we're drifting apart," he said.

"It's just because we don't spend as much time together as we used to."

One of her roommates stuck her head out of the room. "Jessica, we're about to order pizza. You want to go in with us?"

"Yeah, sure."

"What kind do you want?"

"It doesn't matter. Whatever you want."

"We thought about getting one pepperoni and one sausage. Is that okay with you?"

"Sure, that'll be great."

The roommate left.

"Sorry," Jessica said.

"Let's get married this summer."

"We would need to talk about a lot of things before we'd be ready for that."

"Let's talk now then."

Her roommate came back out. "It's going to be three dollars and seventy-nine cents for each of us."

"Okay, hold on a minute." She reached into her pocket and pulled out a five-dollar bill.

"I'll get you change."

A group of seven or eight people coming down the hall recognized Jessica and stopped to talk to her. They were Sioux Indians from North Dakota. Jessica invited them in for pizza. Among themselves they were able to come up with another twenty dollars.

They ended up with about fifteen people sprawled across the beds and on the floor, watching a movie and eating pizza.

Nathan stayed until two o'clock, when he couldn't stay awake any longer. He made his way over people to say good-bye to Jessica, who was talking with the AISES chapter president from North Dakota about a combined activity.

"I'm going to head back to my room," he said.

She came out into the hall with him. "Thanks for sticking around. It means a lot to me that you feel comfortable here with all my friends."

"No problem."

"This weekend is very important to me. You know that, don't you?" she said.

"I know."

She looked down the hall both ways and then kissed him on the cheek. "I'm so glad you came here this weekend. Maybe it will help you understand me better."

It was the wrong time and the wrong place, but he had to say it anyway. "Will you marry me?"

"Let's not rush into anything, okay? We've been through a lot. I think we both need some time before we make a decision like that."

The next morning when he woke up, he closed his eyes and returned to his fantasy. It was long ago and he was on horseback. He came around a bend in the trail and there Jessica was, wearing white buckskin and moccasins. He got down off his horse and, without a word, he and Jessica looked into each other's eyes, and then he kissed her. And then, for the first time since he had been reliving the dream, he led his horse and followed Jessica into the woods to her tepee and stayed with her and her people from then on.

At noon Jessica left in a school van with the rest of the AISES group from South Dakota. Nathan went to church in the afternoon, then drove to Seattle and stayed with a family he had taught and baptized on his mission. The next day he spent time with Mrs. Gibbs. They talked mostly about her husband. Nathan gave her what was left of the money her husband had given him when he first went into hiding.

▼ ▼ ▼

Nathan didn't want anyone to know that he continued to be bothered by bad dreams long after his ordeal was over. The dreams always ended with him being unable to stop Steiger. If he had a gun, either it wouldn't fire or it would fall apart when he pulled the trigger. If in his dream Steiger was choking Jessica and Nathan was trying to get him to stop, Steiger was too strong and easily pushed him away. Sometimes he dreamed he was home when the doorbell rang. When he opened the door, Steiger would be standing there with a gun in his hand; he had come to kill Nathan and his family.

Nathan bought a rifle to protect himself. Sometimes, after waking up from one of those dreams, he'd go outside and sit by the side of the house with the loaded rifle in his hands.

One morning a few days before Thanksgiving, his mother was letting their cat out at four-thirty in the morning when she happened to see him standing guard. She asked what he was doing. He knew if he answered truthfully, she'd insist he get counseling. So he told her he thought he'd heard a dog going through the trash.

"We don't shoot dogs for doing that here," she responded, almost immediately regretting that she'd thrown in the word *here.*

The next day, true to form, his mother suggested that he go for counseling.

"I'm all right," Nathan said. "I just need a little time, that's all."

▼ ▼ ▼

*December*

On the first Friday in December, Nathan saw Camille in the library studying. He asked if he could sit with her. She said yes, but she was all business so they didn't talk much. He found himself glancing up to look at her, though. It rested his eyes. When he looked at her, she made it a point to keep her eyes on the book she was reading. But there were times when he knew she was secretly looking at him too.

They stayed until the library closed. "Can I give you a ride home?" he asked.

"It's not far. I can walk."

"Can I walk you home then?"

"I guess so."

Just before they got to her apartment, he said, "I think my mom would like us to do something together . . . sometime."

"And what do *you* think about that?" she asked.

"I guess it'd be all right—just as friends, of course."

"Yes, of course," she said.

"We could go cross-country skiing near West Yellowstone," he said. "Of course, if that's too much of a challenge for you, we could always just go to a movie." He was smiling as he said it.

Her eyes, usually calm, flashed like a summer storm. "Cross-country skiing will be just fine."

▼ ▼ ▼

On Saturday they left a little after nine in the morning. At the AISES convention in November, Nathan had bought some tapes of powwow songs. The words were in Lakota. He played the music for Camille, but just listening to it made him melancholy.

He wished Jessica were next to him instead of Camille. He remembered the way the light from a fire played across her face.

In his mind he went back in time. It was early in the morning. He and Jessica were just outside Washington, D.C. In a few minutes they would leave to meet with Senator Montgomery. They were together in the backseat of the Jimmy, holding each other, trying to keep their fear from overwhelming them. That was when he'd first talked to her about their getting married, and she'd told him she thought it would be wonderful to be married to him.

The sound of Camille clearing her throat brought him back to reality. He realized he hadn't spoken for a long time. He needed to say something. He glanced over at her. She looked so white and pale compared to Jessica. Before he could think, he blurted out, "Do you get very tan in the summer?"

"Not very."

"This summer when I was with Jessica on her reservation, I got really tan. Some people thought I was American Indian."

"That's all pretty much faded away now, though, hasn't it?"

He glared at her.

"I meant the tan," she said.

"Oh. Yeah, well, maybe so. Sometimes I wish I were an Indian."

"Why?"

"Because that's what Jessica is."

"You miss her a lot, don't you," she said.

"Yeah, I do. We prayed together, we read the Book of Mormon together, we fasted together. I baptized and confirmed her. We ended up driving clear across the country. We almost died together. When I close my eyes, I see her face." He stopped. "I'm boring you with all this, aren't I."

"No, not at all. How does she feel about you?"

"She told me once that I'll always be her hero."

"Do you think the two of you will get married someday?"

"I don't know."

"What's the problem?"

"I'm not sure I could ever get her to leave South Dakota."

"Why not?" she asked.

"She wants to help her people."

"But she'd go wherever you went if she married you, wouldn't she?"

"I'm not sure."

"What are you going to do, then?"

"I've been thinking about telling my dad not to plan on me farming with him."

"You like farming though, don't you." It was a statement rather than a question.

He paused, then said, "That's all I've ever wanted to do. And my dad wants me to take over the farm when he retires."

"Are you willing to give that up for Jessica?"

"Yeah, maybe. I think I might be able to do some good on the reservation."

"What would you do there?" she asked.

He shrugged his shoulders. "I don't know. Teach, maybe."

"I hate to be critical, but can't you find a cause a little closer to home?" she said.

"You don't know what it was like for me there. It was like I'd become an Indian and suddenly the world looked totally different."

"In what way?"

"I didn't realize how much prejudice there is. It's all around us and most of the time we don't even recognize it."

"Okay, great, but isn't there any prejudice around here to work on? Why do you have to go clear back to South Dakota?"

"You don't understand," he said.

"You're right about that. I'll tell you something else I don't understand, and that's why you're willing to throw away your own heritage. If you were an Indian, I could understand you wanting to honor that heritage. But you're not. You're like me. You have ancestors who joined the Church in Europe and traveled to America. And yet right now you seem embarrassed by your own roots. You're right. I don't get it."

"Maybe that's because you're prejudiced against Indians," he said, a little defensively.

"I don't think I am. You do understand, though, that you're not Indian, don't you?"

"I know that."

"Good, I wasn't sure. I think every person should take pride in their own heritage—Jessica in hers, and you in yours."

"If I go back to the reservation, I think I can make a difference."

"You do?"

"Yes."

"Why do you think you can change things back there?" she asked. "Because you're white? Isn't that in itself a racist attitude?"

"I don't care what you say. I know I can make it a little better there."

"Why don't you see what you can do here first, before you abandon your family and your heritage and run off someplace else."

He pulled off to the side of the road to turn around. "Look, I can see now that this was a big mistake. Let me take you home."

She put her hand on the steering wheel. "Nathan, I'm not your enemy. In fact, I may even be your friend. At least I'm not afraid to level with you. Everyone else is tiptoeing around like they were stepping on eggshells. Look, how about if we both promise not to talk about this anymore today? We've already rented the skis—why don't we just go ahead and use them like we planned?"

"All right."

For the rest of the way, she talked about growing up on her family's farm. She had several brothers, so they did most of the work outside. She had grown up helping her mother around the place. From the time she was twelve, she had been in charge of the family garden. It was from her mother that she had learned to love music.

She talked at length about how much she admired Nathan's mother. She told him things about his mother he had never known. He had never seen her in any other role than as the woman who cooked his food and did his laundry. After listening to Camille, he realized that he had always taken his mother's love of music for granted. He had never appreciated how gifted she was.

They stopped in West Yellowstone for hot chocolate. Then they drove a few miles out of town to the beginning of the Madison River Loop cross-country trail. He pulled their skis and poles from the back of his pickup, showed her how to put on the skis, reached into the pickup for the daypack that contained food and water for their trip, and gave Camille a short lesson on cross-country skiing. Finally they set off down the trail.

Because it was her first time cross-country skiing, he figured she'd slow him up, but within a few minutes she was able to maintain a pace that was comfortable for both of them.

It was a cold, sunny day without a cloud in the sky. It had snowed the day before, and on some parts of the trail, they were the first ones there. Looking back, they could see the marks their skis had made in the snow. The more they skied, the warmer they got, and before long they had shed their sweatshirts and tied them around their waists.

He stopped every few minutes to check on how she was doing. She was always ready to press on, and if she was getting tired, she never admitted it. He wondered if that stubbornness came from growing up on a farm. Maybe so, because he was stubborn too. The more time he spent with her, the better she looked to him. He wasn't sure if it was because the cold had made her cheeks rosy or because being outdoors in the snow was cheering him up.

Once she fell down and when he tried to help her up, he lost his balance and fell down too. They lay in the snow giggling like little children. Her eyes sparkled and her breath made tiny clouds when she laughed. And when she laughed, maybe because of her voice training, the sound was musical. He found himself beginning to enjoy her smile, with sparkling white teeth showing, and the way she laughed.

They talked for a while about their memories of growing up—the first time their fathers let them drive a tractor, the first time they realized that not everyone in their schools had chores to do like they did, the first time they realized that everything depended on the crop. They had each been raised in a family where a good year brought a new TV and a bad year made it so they couldn't afford some of the things their friends in school took for granted.

On the drive home, they sang country-western songs. No matter how hard she tried to get a twang into her voice, she still made the songs sound like classical music. But he admired her for trying.

After a while she curled up in her seat and closed her eyes. She seemed very comfortable being with him.

Half an hour from Rexburg, Camille woke up. She stretched like a little kid, enthusiastically lifting up her arms until they touched the roof of the car. "I feel great! How about you?"

"Doing okay."

She noticed his hair was messed up. Using her fingers like a comb, she began to style his hair. She had long delicate fingers and her touch was gentle.

At her apartment, when he pulled in to let her off, he said, "This has been a lot of fun."

"It really has. Usually there's a reason when a mother tries to recruit someone to go out with her son, but you're almost as nice as she said you were."

"What exactly *did* she say about me?" he asked.

"Let's see . . . that you were trustworthy, loyal, thrifty, brave, clean, and reverent. I can't remember the others, but I'm pretty sure there were twelve attributes."

"I'm sorry you've had to put up with that," Nathan said.

"It hasn't been that bad. My roommates and I all enjoyed going through your scrapbook. We thought you were an adorable baby. We especially enjoyed the picture taken right after your bath."

"Oh, my gosh," he groaned. "Is she doing this with all her voice students? What does she do, give a discount to anyone who agrees to go out with me?"

"Not really. I think she's pretty much confining this to me."

"Why just you?"

"You'd better ask her."

Nathan couldn't leave it at that. "Tell me what she's told you about me."

"I don't think I should."

"Why not?" he asked.

"You might get mad."

"Did she say something about you and me?" he persisted. "What was it?"

"Really, I'd rather not get into this."

"Let me guess. Was it something like—she thinks we're *supposed* to get married?"

"Something like that," she said.

"I can't believe it! Is that why you went out with me?"

"I went out with you because I wanted to see what you were like."

"And?"

"I think we could be friends. What do you think?" she asked.

"Yeah, I think so, but I've really got to talk to my mom."

After dropping Camille off, he drove straight home. He found his mother in the kitchen. "Mom, look, I really don't need you going around trying to find a wife for me," he said. "I can't believe you gave Camille my scrapbook and told her you thought she and I should get married."

His mother apologized. Later that night she told him, "Nathan, if you are really serious about Jessica, ask her to come out and spend a few days. I'm sure you both have a lot to talk about. And she needs to get to know us so she'll feel comfortable around us. Tell her we'll pay for the plane ticket."

# CHAPTER THIRTEEN

*Boston, Massachusetts: December 25*

TODD DONOVAN SAT ALONE IN HIS APARTMENT MOST OF THE DAY. He had tried to arrange to be with someone for Christmas, but nobody wanted him. After she filed for divorce, his mother had moved in with her parents in Cleveland. The second week she was there, she had met a dentist named Sheldon Luckhart at a piano concert. His wife had died a year and a half before. When Todd called to see if he could spend Christmas with her, she said she had already made plans.

"What kind of plans?" he asked.

"Sheldon has asked me to go with him and his two daughters to Hawaii for Christmas."

"What about Dad?"

"If you want to go visit him in jail on Christmas Day, go right ahead, but I can't do that. I'll never forgive him for allowing illegal drugs to come into Seattle. How many lives were ruined because of those drugs? I'm sorry, but I don't want to be married to a man like that. As soon as the divorce is final, I'm going to marry Sheldon. Why don't you call Elizabeth and see what she's doing for Christmas?"

His sister, Elizabeth, also discouraged him from visiting her. Now that she was in graduate school, she said she had to work every day of the Christmas holidays on her doctoral dissertation.

His girlfriend, Bridget, did not invite him to spend Christmas with her either. Todd wondered if it was because her parents were concerned about all the bad publicity about his father.

In the afternoon, as he warmed a can of soup, Todd looked outside and saw the family from next door pulling their children on a new sled. They were having fun, but he was all alone.

*I don't have a family anymore,* he thought.

▼ ▼ ▼

*Idaho Falls, Idaho: January 8*

As Jessica got off the small shuttle plane and walked across the gray slush caused by a January thaw, Nathan's first reaction was how Indian she looked. In South Dakota he had grown so used to being around her all the time that whites began to look pale and anemic. But while he'd been home, he'd forgotten how dark she was.

Her smile faded when she saw the expression on his face. *She can tell,* he thought. He wasn't sure whether to give her a hug or shake her hand. She solved that by handing him a large bag to carry.

"What's this?" he asked.

"A present for your family. It's a star quilt."

"That you made?"

"Yeah, sure, why?"

"You didn't need to go to so much work."

"That's how I was raised."

Any awkwardness between them was reduced by the graciousness of his parents. His mother opened her arms and hugged Jessica. "Thank you for saving my son's life," she said. It was a long and tearful embrace.

His father was next. It began as a handshake, but, continuing to hold Jessica's hand, he said, "All the time Nathan was gone, we prayed for his safety. Nathan has told us how much you did for him. You were the answer to our prayers. I feel certain he'd be dead now if it weren't for you. We'll always be grateful to you."

"Nathan taught me so much. Thank you for being such good examples for him."

"Shall we go get your luggage?" Boyd asked.

As they left the terminal, his parents went first together, and then Nathan, and then Kim and Jessica. Jessica noticed the sign welcoming visitors to Idaho Falls, written in several languages. "They left out American Indian," she said to Kim.

"How do you say that in Indian?" Kim asked.

*"How kola."*

"Cool," Kim said. "Can I ask you a question? Are you always this tan?"

"In the summer I'm even darker."

"I'd die to look the way you do."

Jessica smiled. "You should have seen Nathan this summer. He was as dark as me."

"Yes, but that was just a farmer's tan. Besides, now he's totally white again."

"You know, I think you're right," Jessica said.

Nathan felt the barb in Jessica's comment. She was right. There was a difference in him now. He hadn't known it until he saw her step off the plane.

The next day Nathan took Jessica to Wal-Mart to get something for his mom. As they entered the store, he found himself wondering about how people might react to his being with Jessica.

He remembered back a long time ago. It was during one summer and he was working on his dad's farm. He must have been only thirteen and didn't know much, so his father had him work with a man who helped out during the busy months. Nathan and the farmhand were sitting in a pickup in a parking lot when they saw a white man and his Hispanic wife and newborn baby. "I bet he got her pregnant and then had to marry her," the man had said. "That's how those things usually go."

At the time Nathan had accepted what the man had said, but now he knew it had been an ignorant racist comment. Even so, he wondered what people would think when they saw him and Jessica together.

They ran into a girl he had dated in high school. She saw Nathan first and then Jessica.

"Nathan, hi. How's it going?" the girl called out.

"Going good." Nathan would have introduced Jessica, but his mind kind of went blank and he couldn't remember the girl's name. He knew he should have remembered it, because he had dated her a couple of times.

"You two just picking up a few things?"

"Yeah, for my mother," Nathan said.

"Well, I'll see you guys later."

When they were back in his pickup, Jessica asked, "Are you ashamed to be seen with me?"

"No."

"Then why didn't you introduce me to that girl?"

"I couldn't remember her name."

"Oh, c'mon, Nathan, you really expect me to believe that?"

"It's the truth."

"You're not comfortable having me here with your white friends, are you."

Nathan tossed it off. "It's not that."

"What is it, then?"

"It's nothing."

"You think I'm being too sensitive again, is that it?" she asked with an edge in her voice.

"There's no way I'd ever be ashamed of being with you."

They drove back to the house and took in the things they'd bought. Then Nathan told his mother he was going to take Jessica out to show her the farm and that they would be gone for a while.

After arriving at the farm, they went first into one of the potato cellars. He showed her the air-circulation system and explained how important it is to maintain the proper temperature and humidity. Then they went up a flight of stairs and walked out on the pile of potatoes, and he showed her how they were healing from whatever bruises they had received in harvesting. Next they went into a large equipment storage shed. He described how potatoes were harvested. He helped her climb into the huge high-tech grain combine. She was surprised that it was air-conditioned and even equipped with a tape deck.

"There's a lot to farming, isn't there?"

"Yeah, quite a bit. People sometimes talk about 'dumb farmers,' but I'll tell you something—farmers are some of the smartest people around. To be successful, you have to know all about agronomy, electricity, engines, budgeting, markets—everything. This is not like just another job. When my dad took over this place, it needed a lot of work. He's turned it into one of the best-producing farms in this area. Of course, he'd like it to continue in the family. But I've taken too much time showing you around. Let's get out of here. You must be freezing."

"Just my feet."

"You should have said something."

"I was enjoying it. Your face lights up when you talk about this. You must really like it."

"Yeah, I do, very much."

"Is this what you're going to do after you finish college?" she asked.

"I don't know. My dad talks about having me take over the place in a few years. He and Mom want to serve a mission as soon as Kim is through school."

"So if you do take over the farm, it means you're pretty much going to stay in Idaho from now on," she said.

"If I do what my dad wants me to do, but I'm not sure at this point if that's what I want to do."

"I think it's good for a person to do what's in his heart to do. That's why I want to spend the rest of my life working on the reservation. What I'm hoping is that after I graduate, I can work for a couple of years in industry and then see about going back to the School of Mines and being in charge of a minority engineering program there. They need a lot more Indian role models. At least that's what I'm hoping for now."

"That's real good," he said with little enthusiasm.

"Looks like we're going in different directions, doesn't it?" she observed.

"Looks that way."

He was frustrated that she was still determined to stay in South Dakota. He had hoped that her coming to Idaho might help change her mind. "Why did you even come out here anyway?" he asked.

"I came because your mom invited me."

"I thought I invited you."

She looked embarrassed. "Oh, right, that's what I meant."

"Did my mom call you before I did?" he asked.

"Yes."

"Why?"

"She's worried about you," she said. "She said you seem lost. Are you?"

"Yeah, I guess I am."

"That's not unusual, considering all you've been through. She says she's been reading about post-traumatic stress disorder. She thinks you might need some counseling."

"I don't need anything. I'm fine, really."

"Nathan, standing guard outside your house at night is not normal," Jessica said.

"I don't stay out there all night."

"How long?"

"Just a couple of hours, starting about two in the morning."

"They're all in jail, Nathan."

"Maybe there's someone else that we don't know about."

"Nathan, there isn't. It's over."

"I know that. Let's not talk about that anymore. Listen to me. I could walk away from this farm tomorrow and not think a thing about it. And I'll do it, too, if you'll marry me. I'd be real happy to come and live in South Dakota with you."

For some strange reason, he was talking too fast. He remembered feeling that way once before, when he was eight, trying to talk his mom into letting him get a dog. He wondered how long he could stand not farming with his dad. It still was the only thing he wanted to do. Maybe if they did get married, eventually he'd be able to talk Jessica into moving back to Idaho.

"What would you do in South Dakota?" she asked.

"I don't know, but I'm sure I'd find something."

"And you could just give up ever being able to take over your dad's farm?"

"I'd do anything for you, you know that," he said. "I love you. That's all that matters."

"I love you too, Nathan, and I always will, no matter what."

"If you love me, let's get married."

"Just like that?"

"Yeah, sure, why not?"

"Maybe we should just think about it for a while. Okay?"

They had spent so much time together that he could almost read her thoughts. He knew she was trying very hard not to hurt his feelings. "If you love me like you say you do, what's there to think about?" he asked.

"We might get married, Nathan, but if we do, let's at least go into it with our eyes open."

"What are you talking about?"

"In case you haven't noticed, you're white and I'm Indian."

"Hey, if that's the only hangup, if you want, I'll become Indian."

She smiled. "Really? And how are you going to manage that?"

"I'll get myself one of those ethnic transplant operations. I just read about 'em."

She touched his cheek. "I wish you could. You'd make a wonderful 'Skin."

"What difference does any of this make as long as we love each other?" he asked.

"I'm not saying there'd be a problem. All I'm saying is we need to talk."

From his own mother Nathan had learned to look out whenever a woman said "We need to talk." He had the feeling that everything was going down the drain, and none of it made any sense because he loved Jessica more than anyone else in the world.

It was his turn now. "All right, if you want to talk, let's talk. Why couldn't you live here in Idaho once we got married?"

"Because I need to help my people." She said it slowly and with determination.

"There are Indians around here too, you know," he said. "Fort Hall is just down the road."

"Back home they'll listen to me because I'm one of them. And when I go to their schools and tell those kids to stay in school and then go on to college, some of them will believe me, and they'll do it, and that's what I want. I can make a difference there, don't you see? This is something I've got to do. I have a heritage I need to honor—but so do you. I think it would be a mistake for you to leave this farm when it's obvious you love it so much."

"You're more important to me than a few acres of land," he said.

"You can say that now, but would you say it ten years from now?"

He wasn't about to admit the truth to her. "Yes."

She knew him too well. "You don't know that for sure."

"I know that I love you. Why isn't that enough?"

"I don't know. Something's holding me back."

They sat there mute, separate, and discouraged. Nathan didn't want to talk anymore. "Let's head back. My folks will wonder what happened to us."

▼ ▼ ▼

By the time they got home, Nathan's brothers and their wives and families had arrived from Utah. His parents had invited them so they'd have a chance to meet Jessica. Camille was there too. She had volunteered to help Nathan's mother prepare dinner, and Elaine had invited her to stay and eat with the family. Nathan barely acknowledged her presence. He would have been happy if she had never surfaced, but his mother made it a point before they sat down to eat to introduce her to the family and Jessica. He studied Camille's reaction as she met Jessica for the first time. Nathan was surprised, but the two young women greeted each other warmly and seemed immediately to be at ease with each other.

During the meal things seemed to be going well until his brother John, commenting about Jessica being in college, said, "I understand Indians don't have to pay anything to go to college. Is that true?"

"Not from my experience. Of the seventy-five American Indian students at the School of Mines, at least sixty are working part-time during school to pay their expenses."

"Really?" John said. "I must have been told wrong. What are you majoring in?"

"Mechanical engineering."

"I thought it would be in art. I mean . . . everyone knows how talented Indians are . . . you know . . . in pottery and moccasins and things like that."

"We can do other things too," Jessica said.

"John," his wife said, hoping to get him to stop.

"How can I learn unless I ask?" John replied. Turning to Jessica, he said, "I hope you don't mind me asking questions."

"Not really."

John went on. "Here's something else I don't understand. I saw you on TV complaining about the names of certain teams— you know, like the Washington Redskins and the Atlanta Braves. I still don't understand why that's offensive to Native Americans."

"Because it promotes negative stereotypes."

"I don't think it's negative," he said.

"You're probably not the most qualified to judge what's offensive to an Indian, are you?" Jessica said.

Andrew slowly nodded and muttered under his breath, "Probably not."

"Would anyone care for dessert?" Elaine jumped in, seeing her chance to defuse the bomb that seemed about to go off at her supper table.

"Just a minute. I've got one more question," John said. "Nathan tells us he danced at a powwow once."

"Yes, he did."

"I've heard about powwows, but I've never been to one," John went on. "What's so important about powwows?"

"The feeling that we're all one. It's one of the last ways we have left to gather together and learn about each other. It's a place of respect and honor for everyone."

Andrew had been listening uncomfortably to his brother's interrogation of Jessica. In an effort to relieve the tension, he said,

"If you two do get married, I bet you'll end up loving Idaho as much as we do. It's really a great place to live and raise a family. We've got some of the greatest mountains and rivers and lakes in the world."

"Actually, we're not sure we'd live here," Nathan said.

"Where would you live?" Andrew asked.

"Maybe South Dakota."

"On an Indian reservation?" Andrew's wife asked.

"Yeah, probably," Nathan said.

"I thought you were going to take over the farm," John said.

"I was, but I'm not sure anymore," Nathan said. He regretted not having talked to his father before this.

"You're thinking of not helping your father?" his mother asked.

"We're talking about a lot of things right now, but we haven't made any decisions yet," Nathan said, knowing that his father would be hurt that he hadn't at least talked to him about this before.

Elaine and Camille got up to clear the dishes off the table. One of John's children asked Jessica to tell them about Indians, and she gladly agreed. She and the children went into the TV room. From the dining room, Nathan could see them there, with the children sitting on the floor around Jessica, listening to her with rapt attention.

Because Andrew and John had to be at work the next day, about half an hour later they started to get their families ready to go. Before they left, his mother insisted they take pictures. Nathan's father had always been the official family photographer, and he was very seldom in any of their pictures. Tonight Elaine asked Camille to come and take pictures.

After Camille had snapped every possible grouping there could be, Boyd suggested that she take a picture of just Nathan and Jessica together.

Nathan felt awkward having Camille there as if she were part of the family when she clearly wasn't. But just before she took their picture, he put his arm around Jessica and pulled her to him and kissed her on the cheek. Camille took the picture before Jessica could pull away.

Jessica glared at him. "Don't ever do that again," she whispered.

"What'd I do wrong now?" he asked.

"I was brought up not to show affection in public. Besides that, it was like you were trying to establish possession . . . you know, like 'This is my woman.'"

"Sorry."

Before leaving, John made a point of thanking Jessica for answering his questions. "I feel like I need to wipe the slate clean and start all over," he said, shaking her hand.

"We can all learn from each other," Jessica responded. Nathan wished she had smiled a little more warmly as she said it.

After Andrew and John and their families left, Jessica and Camille volunteered to do the dishes and they ran everyone else out of the kitchen, including Nathan. After they finished, the two young women left together because Jessica wanted to see Camille's apartment.

They were gone an hour and a half. When they came back, Jessica's hair was braided into a thick ponytail. She said that Camille had done it for her while they talked.

Nathan teased Camille. "You just can't keep your hands out of other people's hair, can you."

"She's really nice. I can see why you like her so much."

"Thanks."

After everyone had left or gone to bed, Nathan and Jessica were alone in the living room. "Let's talk about what happened in Wal-Mart today," she said.

Things were definitely going downhill. He wished that someday he'd find a woman who never needed to talk to him about anything.

Jessica went on. "Maybe you didn't realize it at the time, but I had the definite feeling that you were ashamed to be seen in public with me."

"I will never be ashamed to be seen with you in public."

"All right, *ashamed* may be too strong a word. Let's just say that you were self-conscious about being seen with an Indian. There, is that better?"

"Maybe," he said.

"Why? Was it because of things you've heard people say?"

"I could see it in their faces, the way they looked at us," he said.

"I saw it in their eyes—but I saw it in yours too."

"We can work this out," he said.

"Are you sure?" she asked. "There are so many things we need to talk about. If we get married, are our children going to be raised white or Indian? What are we going to do when we find out we have totally different ideas about raising children? What are you going to do when I want to take our children to powwows so they can learn to appreciate their Indian heritage? What is it going to be like if kids in school make fun of our kids? Even if we live here, what if I decide to take our children home in the summer but you want them to work on the farm? What if I can't stand living here among so many whites? Or, if we live on the reservation, what if after a while you can't stand it there? And if I marry you, our kids won't be accepted as much among my people because they'll be half-breeds. Maybe they'll even be confused about who they are. What if they're not fully accepted in either white or Indian society? Do we want to put that kind of burden on our children?"

"Why does this have to get in the way?" he asked. "The fact that we're in love should be all that matters."

"Maybe that *is* all that matters. To tell you the truth, I don't know. I just know we need to talk it all out so there are no surprises."

He got ready for bed first. By the time he was in bed, he could hear her running the water in the bathroom. On her way to the guest bedroom, she knocked on his door. "Nathan?"

"Come in."

She stuck her head in the door. "I really do love you, and I always will. I just don't know what to do with it."

He sat up in bed and turned on the light next to his bed. "Why don't you come in for a while, so we can talk some more."

She shook her head. "Your mom and dad wouldn't want us to be alone in your room this late at night."

"It wouldn't matter. We have great self-discipline."

"I'm not so sure we can depend on that anymore. Goodnight, Nathan. I love you."

"I love you too." She looked at him with a sad expression on her face and returned to her room.

The next morning he drove her to the airport. Nothing had been resolved by the visit.

▼ ▼ ▼

On the Saturday after Jessica left, Kim coaxed Nathan into taking her skiing. On the way back, she said, "You're really messed up, aren't you."

"Am I?"

"Take it from me—you are. Totally messed up."

"In what way?"

"Gosh, I don't even know where to begin." She let out a big sigh. "Let's start with Jessica. The way I see it, you served a twenty-five-month mission, and she was one of your converts. That's all. Why make it into something it's not?"

"There's more to it than that."

"I don't see it. You want to know what I think happened when Jessica and Camille went off together on her last night here? I think they worked out a deal."

"What are you talking about?"

"I think Jessica gave you away."

"Why would you think that?" he asked.

"Because they both came back smiling."

"That's crazy."

"Is it? I don't think so."

▼ ▼ ▼

*February*

Donovan and Steiger's trial began the second week in February in Seattle. Nathan and Jessica were subpoenaed to testify. Nathan's mission president invited them to stay in the mission home. They flew in on Saturday, went to church on Sunday, and both of them spoke at a fireside in one of the wards where Nathan had gone to church when he'd been on his mission.

They were needed in court for two days, and then they flew home on different flights. A couple of weeks later Donovan and Steiger were found guilty and later sentenced to life in prison.

Nathan and Jessica were also called to testify at Senator Montgomery's trial in the District of Columbia the last week in February. A blizzard in South Dakota grounded all planes and prevented Jessica from getting there on the days Nathan testified. She arrived on the day he left to go home. They missed each other by two hours.

Montgomery was found guilty a few days later.

▼ ▼ ▼

The night before his father was to be transferred to a federal penitentiary, Todd Donovan visited him in the county jail. His mother had by that time secured a divorce. Todd was the only one in the family who would have anything to do with his father.

"You're a good son," his father said. "You're the only one left for me—the only one who can pay the two back who put me here."

"I can visit you when I'm in town and I'll always do that—but I won't do what you want me to do."

"Have you dipped into the ice-cream fund?" Jack asked. Todd realized it was his father's way of asking if he'd used any of the money.

"Yes—a little."

"I thought we agreed that if you did that, there were certain things I wanted done."

"I can't do what you want me to do."

"It's not that hard. These days everything is electronic. It's like playing a video game. I have a friend who can teach you everything you need to know."

"Why me?"

"You're using my money, aren't you? Think of it as a family responsibility." Donovan mouthed a name and a phone number. "Either talk to my friend or put yourself through school."

Todd had no intention of killing Nathan and Jessica, but he

was afraid his father would somehow stop him from withdrawing money from the account. He wanted to finish school. Not only that, but he wanted to get a better car so Bridget wouldn't be embarrassed to go out with him.

He decided that as long as he was in college, he would let his father think he was going to kill Nathan and Jessica. And then, when the money was gone, he'd tell his father he couldn't do it.

The next day, after talking to his father's friend over the phone, Todd met with a man who taught him how to assemble a radio-activated car bomb.

When he got back to school, he bought a new car. Bridget loved it.

*March*

In March Jessica attended Lamanite Week at BYU as an invited speaker. Nathan drove down to be with her the last day of the event. By the time he arrived she had been there for two days. He had never seen her happier. She explained she had met two returned sister missionaries who had told her about their missions among the Indians.

"I've been thinking about serving a mission," she said.

"Oh?"

"It might be good for us. It'll give us some time to think. I believe I need that right now in my life, if I'm to do all the things for my people that I'm supposed to do. Nathan, I'm going to pray about it."

Two weeks later she met with her bishop and began preparing her mission papers.

▼ ▼ ▼

"That's it," Nathan said when he heard that Jessica had sent in her mission papers. "From now on I'm through with women."

Two days later his mother suggested he take Camille to the Ricks College production of *My Fair Lady*.

After the play was over, Camille asked him how he liked it. His only comment was, "I liked her better when she was selling flowers."

Camille understood. "I hear Jessica is going on a mission."

He shook his head and sighed. "That's what she says."

"You should be happy about it. Think how much stronger she's going to be."

"I'm not sure I want her any stronger."

"Men," Camille said, shaking her head. "I've been thinking about going on a mission when I turn twenty-one."

"I think you should go. It'd be good for you."

She smiled. "How come every girl you spend time with ends up going on a mission?"

"It's true. Three dates with me and a girl is willing to give up dating for eighteen months. It's probably not a good sign, right?"

"Probably not. What are you going to do about writing all the girls you're getting to serve missions?"

"I don't know—maybe I'll start a newsletter."

She crumpled up her program from the play and threw it at him.

▼ ▼ ▼

In the weeks before Jessica left on her mission, Nathan wrestled with his feelings. At times he didn't think he could stand to have her gone for a year and a half. At other times he could see that it would be good for her to go. And at other times he just wanted to get married—practically anyone would do—and settle down.

▼ ▼ ▼

*Rapid City, South Dakota: July*

Jessica was called to the New Mexico Albuquerque Mission with a special assignment to work with Indians. Nathan attended her farewell in the Rapid City Second Ward, and afterwards they were invited to have lunch with President Burns and his family. He was Jessica's stake president while she was living in Rapid City as a student and would be setting her apart later in the evening.

After lunch they went off by themselves to the TV room downstairs. Nathan found himself in a new role with Jessica— that of missionary trainer. He tried to tell her all he'd learned on his mission. He was sure none of it would make any sense until she was serving full time.

"I'd like to write to you while you're on your mission. Is that all right?" he asked.

"You know it is."

"I'll write good letters. I won't tell you how much I miss you. I won't ask you to marry me. I'll write positive, newsy letters. You'll see."

"Fair enough."

Nathan and Jessica's grandmother were there when Jessica—now Sister Red Willow—was set apart as a missionary. Afterwards, Nathan shook her hand and wished her well.

▼ ▼ ▼

An eighteen-month mission—in the beginning it seemed like an eternity, but eventually Nathan decided he should use the time to also grow and progress. And he did. He got some counseling to help him deal with what had happened to him. He graduated from Ricks College and then transferred to Utah State University, where he majored in agriculture. He spent the summer helping his dad on the farm.

He was true to his word about writing to Jessica. Anyone reading his letters might have assumed he was just a friend. He knew how much she wanted to do a good job as a missionary. She didn't need him whining about how much he missed her.

That fall Camille transferred from Ricks to Idaho State University in Pocatello. She and Nathan managed to see each other about once a month. She was the only woman he could talk to about Jessica; she, in turn, told him about the guys she was dating.

▼ ▼ ▼

One Saturday in June Nathan was pulling a fifty-foot rod-weeder behind the tractor, preparing the field by keeping it free of weeds for planting winter wheat in the fall. A little before noon, he saw Camille walking toward him across the field. He stopped the tractor and opened the door for her. As she climbed up beside him, the first thing he noticed was a beaded Indian medallion around her neck. "I was visiting your mom," she said. "She asked me to bring you your lunch on my way out of town." She handed him a large bag.

"I'm glad you came." He noticed there was more food in the bag than he usually ate. "Want to join me?" he asked.

"Maybe later. Can I drive this rig while you eat?"

He moved over to let her drive. He was impressed that she seemed to know what she was doing. "You've done this before?" he asked.

"Sure, lots of times."

While he ate and she drove, he put on his favorite tape of country-western songs. She sang along. It sounded as if she'd been practicing.

When they came around to where her car was parked, he had her stop. "I need to get out and stretch my legs," he said.

They walked together. "How's Jessica doing?" she asked.

"She's really having a good mission. Everyone loves her. She's having a lot of success."

"I knew she would."

They reached the top of a hill. He pointed out the boundaries of their land.

"It's beautiful," she said.

"I know. Someday I want to have a house up here, so I can look out and see all this." He reached for her hand and together they walked back.

He was reluctant to admit it, but he realized how attracted he was to her. For some reason she was doing everything right today—the way she handled the tractor, the natural way she sang country-western songs, the smell of sagebrush in her hair, the way she looked in jeans and a simple T-shirt.

They sat in her car and talked. And when he looked into her eyes something happened, and he kissed her.

When it was over, they were both a little embarrassed. "I'd better go," she said.

"I guess I'd better get back to work too."

There were many reasons he could think of why he could be happy if he were to marry Camille. She would be a busy home-

making, bread-baking, children-raising, and "just-checking—
have-you-done-your-home-teaching-yet" kind of wife. She would
buy his clothes and coordinate his ties and remind him when he
needed to spend more time with their children. But it wouldn't be
all work. She'd make sure the two of them spent time together,
alone. She'd probably even help with the potato harvest. He knew
he'd always be able to depend on her.

"This might be the last time I see you for a while," she said.
"I'll probably be sending in my mission papers next week." She
seemed to be studying his face to determine his reaction.

Until Jessica returned from her mission, he had nothing to say
that might give Camille a reason to stay home. "I'll be sure and
write you while you're gone," he said.

That was it. Camille's question was answered. It was time to
get on with her life. She smiled. "You'd better."

Just before she left, he said, "About what happened back
there . . . "

She nodded. "I know. It was a mistake. We should have
known better. Sometimes friendship and romance don't mix. I
guess this is one of those times. See you around, Nathan."

"Don't go. There's something I need to tell you."

"What?"

"I really, uh, l-like you," he stammered. The last time he
remembered stammering in front of a girl was in ninth grade.
Why was he doing it now in front of Camille?

"I like you too, Nathan."

"A lot?"

"Yes, a lot."

"The thing is, though, I have to wait for Jessica to get back,"
he said.

"I know you do."

They stood there looking at each other until she said she
needed to leave and he mumbled something about getting back
to work, and he let her go.

In September Camille left on a Spanish-speaking mission to
California.

▼ ▼ ▼

## New Mexico: December

Todd Donovan sat in a rental car, waiting for Jessica Red Willow and her missionary companion to come out of their apartment at the start of another day. He had flown in the night before, rented a car, found the mission car Jessica and her companion were using, and, under cover of darkness, slapped a car bomb with magnetic backing on the frame of the car, just below the driver's seat.

His father was right; it would be easy. All he had to do was push two buttons in sequence, and a radio signal from a transmitter would set off the bomb.

His life was in shambles. Even after he had spent so much money to keep Bridget happy, she had finally left him. He had started drinking and skipping classes. And now he was on the verge of being kicked out of school. He would have to repeat some classes, which meant going another year. He needed more money. And yet the last time he tried to withdraw from the account, Mr. Sullivan informed him that his father had cut him off "until such time as he started to live up to family responsibilities."

That's why he needed to kill Jessica and Nathan.

Jessica and her companion came out of their apartment, got in their car, and drove away. Todd's plan was to follow them until they were on an isolated stretch of highway and then detonate the car bomb.

For some reason the rental car refused to start. Todd tried it several times. Finally it started, and Todd raced to catch up.

A flashing red light appeared in his rearview mirror. He thought of trying to outrun the police car behind him but decided against it. He pulled over. "Anything wrong, officer?" Todd asked.

"You were going forty-one in a twenty-five-mile-an-hour speed zone," the policeman said.

Todd breathed a sigh of relief, grateful that was all it was about. "Sorry."

"I'll need to see your driver's license."

The policeman now had his name and address. Todd knew that because he was a stranger in town, if he killed Jessica and her companion, he would be a prime suspect. His best bet was just to get out of town. Late that night he returned to the apartment where Jessica and her companion lived and removed the bomb from the mission car. The next day he flew back to Boston.

A day later he wrote his father a long letter and told him, using a kind of code that would not alert any prison officials who might read the letter, that he had tried to carry out his father's will but had failed. He complained that Jessica never left her companion's side, and he didn't see what purpose it would serve to kill them both. He also complained that if he killed Jessica and Nathan one at a time in separate instances, it would be easier for him to be caught. He asked his father to let him continue to draw money from the secret bank account until he graduated. He promised that after Jessica finished her mission, he would wait until she and Nathan were together, and then he would kill them both.

His father agreed to free up the account until Jessica returned from her mission.

▼ ▼ ▼

*January–November*

Boyd Williams was beginning to wonder if Nathan was ever going to get married. Whenever Nathan did bring a girl home, Boyd and Elaine always fell in love with her. And then they felt betrayed when he quit seeing her.

Finally Boyd could stand it no more. "How's it going to be any different when Jessica gets home?" he asked Nathan one day after returning home from attending a national potato growers convention.

"It's probably not going to be much different. She won't leave her people."

"Sit down, I want to talk to you," Boyd said, spreading all the printed material he had gathered up at the convention on the kitchen table. For as long as Nathan could remember, all the important family decisions had been made at the kitchen table. "There's something I think we should consider. Are you aware that they grow potatoes in western Nebraska, not too far from the Pine Ridge Reservation?"

They talked about his father helping Nathan get a start farming in Nebraska.

Boyd had never gone into any new venture without first doing extensive research. After potato harvest that year, he and Nathan took a few days off and drove to Nebraska to look around. They talked to potato growers in the area and looked over some farms that were for sale, then decided to wait for the next year's crop to come in before they made any decisions. If they had a good year, they'd look seriously for some land to buy or lease in Nebraska.

Nathan kept quiet about all this in his letters to Jessica. He didn't want to exert any pressure on her while she was on her mission. It wouldn't be fair to make her deal with that and do missionary work too.

"You should at least say something to her about what you're thinking," his mother said.

"No. I want it to be a surprise."

It was that, all right.

# CHAPTER FOURTEEN

*January, eighteen months after Jessica left on her mission*

SISTER JESSICA RED WILLOW SHOOK THE HAND of her mission president, waved to the missionaries who had come to see her off, then turned and presented her ticket to the agent at the gate. After eighteen months she was going home.

Just before boarding the plane, she looked at her ticket; her seat assignment was 17A. She had requested a window seat so she could have one last look at New Mexico.

When she reached row 17, she noticed someone in her seat. "Oh, my gosh!"

"Oh, sorry," Nathan said. "Am I in your seat? Here, I'll move."

He moved to the aisle, let her in to the window seat, and then sat down in the aisle seat. She was more beautiful than ever before. She had the same almost mysterious quality in her eyes and face and hair, which was shorter. But now, there was a radiance and warmth that accentuated her beauty. She was so striking in appearance that Nathan was stunned into silence and found himself staring at her without shame.

She was obviously uncomfortable. "This isn't right, and you know it," she said. "What was true for you after your mission is true for me now. I'm still on my mission until I talk to my stake president."

"Now you know what I was talking about."

"Yes, now I know."

He could hardly keep from laughing. "Let me get this straight. After you've talked with your stake president, then it will be okay for us to be together, is that right?"

"Yes, then it will."

"Great," he said.

She was suspicious. "Why did you say great? What do you mean by *great?*"

"I've grown really close to President Burns in Rapid City. He's a wonderful man."

She looked at him suspiciously. "I know that."

"Did you know he has a sister here in Albuquerque?"

"I didn't know that."

"Well, he does."

At Nathan's nod, President Burns, wearing his usual blue suit, came up the aisle from the back of the plane and stopped at their row. "Excuse me, I believe I'm in the middle seat." Hardly able to contain himself, Nathan stood up to let him sit down.

"Well, have you two been behaving yourselves?" President Burns asked with a smile.

Jessica leaned forward to talk to Nathan. "How did you ever arrange this?"

"President, you tell her."

"I needed to come here anyway. Nathan called me six months ago and told me what he was thinking of doing. Normally I would have said no, but knowing what happened the first time you met, I thought I'd better come along, just in case. And, of course, I really did need to come here to see my sister. We have some property that belonged to our family that we need to sell. So it all worked out."

"I'm going to stay with President Burns's family this weekend so I can hear you speak in sacrament meeting," Nathan said.

"Really?"

He was puzzled by her obvious unease. "Is that okay?" he asked.

"Yes, of course. It's just that . . . you never told me any of this in your letters."

"I thought I'd surprise you."

"If you two will promise to behave, I'll change seats with Nathan," President Burns said.

Nathan and President Burns switched seats.

"You look so good!" Nathan said, looking at Jessica.

"Thanks. Going on a mission was the best thing I ever did. Thanks for your letters," she added. "They were just what I needed."

She asked about Camille.

"The last I heard, she was doing well," Nathan said.

"We've written a few times," Jessica said.

"Really?" Nathan still felt guilty about kissing Camille. "What about?"

"Mainly about our missions. She really likes you, Nathan."

"We're just friends."

"That's what she said too."

After the plane landed in Denver, the three of them walked to another gate to wait for the flight to Rapid City. President Burns stayed nearby so Jessica wouldn't feel uncomfortable being alone with Nathan.

"I can hardly wait to tell you something. I'm pretty sure it'll solve all our problems," Nathan said.

"What?"

"They grow potatoes in Nebraska, not too far from your reservation."

"They do?"

"Yes, and the land isn't too expensive there. Land prices in Idaho are really shooting out of sight now. My dad thought of the idea first. I guess he hated to see me moping around missing you. A few weeks ago we drove to Nebraska and looked around, and we found a place for sale. I think it's going to be real productive land." He paused. "And guess how many miles it is from Pine Ridge?"

"How many?"

"Eighty miles, a little over an hour away. We can have it all, the potatoes for me, you helping on the reservation, and lots of brown-eyed kids of our own. What could be better?"

Her mouth dropped open. "I don't know what to say."

"Don't say anything. My dad and I are closing on the deal next week so I'll be up there. We'll come by and see you then."

"Nathan, you should have told me about this before now."

"I wanted to surprise you."

She wiped her brow. "Well, you sure did that."

"What's wrong?"

"I was going to write you . . . "

"Just tell me."

"I met someone on my mission."

"What do you mean, you met someone on your mission?"

"He was my zone leader. He's from the Sisseton-Wahpeton reservation in northern South Dakota. We have a lot in common."

"You were supposed to be on a mission, not looking for guys."

"Nothing happened. We didn't even talk to each other for more than a few minutes. I heard him give a few talks at zone conferences, and he heard me talk in our testimony meetings. But the thing is that he and I are so much alike. Both of us want to help our people. He's been home from his mission now about four months. He's written to me."

"What's his name?"

"John Eagle Hawk. You'll get to meet him this weekend. He's coming to hear me talk in church."

"He is?"

"Yes."

"Is there anyone else coming I should know about? If there's enough of us, maybe we could form a men's chorus and sing a couple of songs in church in your honor."

"There's just you and him," she said softly.

He looked away, trying to hide his disappointment. When he turned to her again, he did his best to be almost businesslike.

"Maybe I should tell my dad to hold off buying any land in Nebraska."

"I think that might be a good idea until we know for sure what's going to happen."

"You're serious about him?"

"I haven't spent a lot of time thinking about it. I always figured there'd be time to work this out after my mission."

▼ ▼ ▼

When the plane landed in Rapid City, Nathan went with
President Burns to stay with his family. Jessica had arranged to
stay with her aunt in Rapid City.

On Friday Nathan and Jessica drove to the reservation in a
snowstorm. They spent the day visiting her grandmother. On
Saturday night the three of them went to the Pine Ridge Branch
meetinghouse where the members honored Jessica at a supper.
She would have two homecomings. The first would be in Rapid
City the next day; the second would be a week later in the Pine
Ridge Branch.

▼ ▼ ▼

*Rapid City, South Dakota: Sunday*

Todd Donovan, wearing a tie and sportcoat, pulled into the
church parking lot, parked next to the rusty GMC Jimmy that
Jessica had been driving that day, and took a basketball and the
bomb out of his rental car, which he had rented under an assumed
name. He let the ball roll under the Jimmy, then got down on his
knees to look for it and slapped the magnetic bottom of the bomb
onto the frame of the Jimmy. Afterwards, he got up, walked
around the vehicle, and picked up the ball. Anyone observing his
actions would think he had merely been looking for the basketball.

Finding Jessica's schedule had been easy. All he had to do
was call the stake president, say he was an old friend, and explain
that he wanted to hear her speak about her mission. Now he had
only to wait until after the church services were over, follow
Jessica and Nathan until they were in some remote place, push
two buttons, and his debt to his father would be paid off.

His father had recently written him a letter, leading him to
believe he would receive even more money if he succeeded in
killing Jessica and Nathan.

Todd had met a young woman that semester, a senior at
Harvard who had been accepted for graduate school at the

University of Chicago. She kept telling him he should go to graduate school too. He hoped that as soon as he received his bachelor's degree, he could follow her to Chicago. But all of that would require money.

Killing Nathan Williams and Jessica Red Willow wasn't anything personal. It was just something he needed to do to make his dreams come true.

▼ ▼ ▼

By the time Sunday School was over, John Eagle Hawk still had not arrived at the chapel. Nathan could see that Jessica was concerned, so as she was about to go up on the stand for sacrament meeting, he offered to watch for John. Walking out into the parking lot, he saw a young man his age waiting in a car. Thinking that it might possibly be John, he went out to meet him. "Are you here for Jessica Red Willow's homecoming?" Nathan asked.

The stranger seemed a little nervous. Also, he didn't appear to be someone who would have the last name of Eagle Hawk. Nathan thought he might be a nonmember friend of Jessica's from the School of Mines and that he was a little nervous about walking into a church he knew nothing about.

"You look a little nervous. Is this your first time at church?" he asked.

"Yes, it is," the stranger replied.

"If you want, you can sit with me."

Just then a pickup pulled into the parking lot. Nathan looked at the driver, who definitely was Indian. "I think this is the guy I've been waiting for," he said. "You want to come in and sit with us?"

"I don't think so."

"Well, I know this is new to you, but there's nothing to be afraid of. If you just want to hear Jessica, she'll be speaking in about half an hour. You could sneak in the back and sit down and listen to what she has to say. I think you'd really enjoy it."

The stranger nodded. "I might just do that."

Nathan went over to meet John. Under any other circumstances, he would have been impressed by this tall, athletic-looking returned missionary. But with Jessica involved, he didn't appreciate the competition. He reached the pickup just as John got out. He was two inches taller than Nathan. His dark brown hair was still trimmed to meet missionary standards.

"I'm organizing a cheering section for Jessica. Are you John?" Nathan asked.

John looked at him and smiled and nodded. They shook hands. *He's not afraid of competition,* Nathan thought.

With a slight smile, Nathan said, "Looks like this is the day we've both been waiting for. Right?"

"It is for me," John said.

Todd decided it wouldn't hurt to hear what Jessica had to say. Unseen, he slipped into the closed-up overflow area at the rear of the chapel. He was alone and sat there in the dark, listening as the meeting progressed.

In her talk Jessica told about some of the people she had taught who had been baptized and of the changes that had occurred in their lives since then. She concluded: "I used to think education was enough to bring my people to where they could begin to take their place in today's world. And, of course, educa-tion *is* important. We need Indian geologists to determine how and when to use the natural resources found on reservation land. We need Indian engineers to design and build the bridges and dams on our land. We need Indian teachers to teach our children. My people need to take control of their destiny and not leave it in the hands of others. We are the ones who can say what is best for us. That will require education. Today's warriors are the ones who graduate from high school and go on to college."

She paused, searching for the right words, and then contin-ued, "I've always believed that education is important, but on my mission, I learned it's not the only thing we need. The gospel of Jesus Christ is also necessary if my people are to obtain the bless-ings promised us by the Lord.

"The first time I read the Book of Mormon was in a tent at night by the light of a Coleman lantern. It was there that I first learned of the promises made to the Lamanites, of the time to come when Lamanites will accept Jesus Christ as their Savior and, because of that acceptance, become a pure and delightsome people. I saw that happen on my mission as people joined the Church and began to live its teachings. I want to do what I can to help it happen here among my people.

"In my culture we have a word that means 'all my relatives.' We have that feeling in this church about one another. Regardless of the color of our skin or where our ancestors came from, we are all brothers and sisters. You are my brother. You are my sister. We are all children of the same Father in Heaven. We are all in the same family."

Todd Donovan did not like it when people talked about families. What family did he have? His mother was now married to the dentist from Cleveland and didn't seem to want to have Todd around. Maybe he reminded her new husband of how old she was. His sister had turned to academic pursuits to escape the burden of their family's disgrace. She also had no time for Todd. His father's only interest in Todd was to get him to enforce a warped sense of family honor.

He was all alone. So how was it that a woman he didn't even know could say she was his sister, and somehow make him feel it was true?

It didn't make sense.

▼ ▼ ▼

During the closing hymn, Nathan returned to the daydream he had entertained about Jessica since the very beginning. He was on horseback and, coming around a bend in the trail, he saw her, alone, dressed in white buckskin, standing on the trail. He stopped and they looked into each other's eyes. Always before, he had gotten down off his horse and they had embraced. Then he would ask her to come with him, and she would climb up behind him on the horse and they would ride off together. But this time his daydream was different. When he met her she also was on a horse. And this time she wasn't alone. Standing beside her were the chiefs and warriors of long ago, wearing their ancient headdresses. They seemed to be waiting for her.

*She might just do it,* he thought. *She might become the kind of a leader for her people that her ancestors will someday honor. Maybe introducing her to the gospel will turn out to be the most important part of my mission. She belongs here with someone like John by her side. Together they can help their people.*

The first thing Nathan said to John after the benediction was, "How serious are you about Jessica?"

"Very serious," John said. "What about you?"

"I will always care about her."

John nodded. "She feels the same way about you."

"But I'm waiting for a missionary," Nathan added suddenly.

"I didn't know that. How long have you been waiting for her?"

Nathan looked at his watch. "Two minutes."

John and Nathan watched Jessica as she talked with people after the meeting. She looked more beautiful and animated to Nathan than ever before. He knew he would never forget her or what she had given him. The memory of her natural beauty and innate dignity would always stay with him.

Nathan came up to her on the stand after everyone else had left, except for John, who was sitting alone near the back of the chapel, patiently waiting for Jessica.

He reached out for her hand and held it and looked into her eyes. "I loved your talk."

"Thank you." There was a muted sadness in her eyes.

"And I'm glad I got a chance to meet John. He seems like a nice guy."

"He is."

"Has he asked you to marry him yet?"

"Not yet."

"He'll get around to it."

She nodded. He knew she didn't want to hurt his feelings.

"Do you love him?" he asked.

"He and I need to get to know each other better." She paused. "But it's looking good so far."

"I really think you'd be good together. We both need to follow our dreams. You want to stay here. I want to spend my life in Idaho on a farm putting little Band-Aids on bruised potatoes."

Though her eyes were glistening with tears, she smiled. "I suppose somebody has to do that."

"I've decided to wait for Camille—if she'll have me."

"She'll have you."

"How do you know?"

"We've kept in touch. She knows all about John."

Todd Donovan sat alone in the overflow area as the meeting ended. He was puzzled by the unusual feelings he had experienced while listening to Jessica. He wasn't sure what it all meant, but something had happened to him during that meeting.

*I don't have to do this,* he thought. And the wave of relief that came over him was so strong that he decided to go with the impulse and remove the car bomb.

He hurried outside to the parking lot. He dropped to his hands and knees where the Jimmy was parked and reached for the bomb.

"Car trouble?" asked a man who had come from the meeting.

"No. Just checking something," Todd told him.

"Because if you need any help, I'm a mechanic," the man said.

"I don't need any help." Todd stood up and smiled. "I'm all done. Thanks anyway."

The man nodded and continued on to his car. Todd went back inside the building to wait for the man to leave. As soon as the parking lot was clear for a moment, even though there were still people inside the building, he ran back out, removed the car bomb from the Jimmy, and drove away.

That night before turning in his rental car at the airport, he drove to a deserted area and detonated the car bomb. He realized now that he had no responsibility to give into his father's insane demands. The first thing he had to do was get himself straightened out. After that, he'd try to find out what Jessica had meant when she said they were all part of the same family.

On his way home, Nathan had a two-hour layover at the Salt Lake City airport. Because he was tired of sitting, he paced up and down the concourse, waiting for his flight to Idaho Falls to be called. As he passed the monitors showing incoming and outgoing flights, he saw a Hispanic man and his wife and a little girl who looked to be about eight years old. The girl was trying to make sense of the flight information. Her father was holding their tickets in his hand but upside down. They were speaking in Spanish.

Nathan stopped. Suddenly the entire scene became clear to him. Hundreds of people were pouring past this little family, all of them unaware, unseeing, uncaring.

Even though there was now no chance that he and Jessica would marry, and even though his South Dakota tan had long ago faded, Nathan realized one thing: a part of him would always be earth-tone brown. It was Jessica's gift.

"Excuse me, little girl," he asked. "Does your family need any help?"

The girl said something in Spanish to her father, who nodded his head, smiled, and handed the tickets to Nathan. Nathan checked the monitor and discovered that their flight was boarding on the next concourse. He walked to the gate with them and waited until they got on their plane, then hurried off to catch his own flight.

He barely made it. He presented his ticket and went to his seat.

Nathan finally was going home.